Creat[illegible]es

Incy Wincy Spider

No one was there to watch the computer. No one saw the screen start to glow with a strange greeny-blue light. It shouldn't have been possible. The computer was switched off. But it happened. And at the heart of the glow was a single black dot. The dot expanded till it was about the size of an egg. Then suddenly it, and the eerie glow, vanished.

Half a minute later, there was a tiny little scratching, scrabbling noise. And from the back of the machine, a *thing* emerged. It was very small. It didn't have much of a shape.

But it did have a lot of legs. . .

Look for other Creatures titles by Louise Cooper:

1 Once I Caught a Fish Alive
2 If You Go Down to the Woods
3 See How They Run
4 Who's Been Sitting in My Chair?
5 Atishoo! Atishoo! All Fall Down!
6 Give a Dog a Bone
7 Daddy's Gone A-Hunting

Creatures at Christmas

Creatures

Incy Wincy Spider

Louise Cooper

Scholastic Children's Books
Commonwealth House, 1–19 New Oxford Street,
London WC1A 1NU, UK
London ~ New York ~ Toronto ~ Sydney ~ Auckland
Mexico City ~ New Delhi ~ Hong Kong

First published by Scholastic Ltd, 2000

ISBN 0 439 01289 9

Typeset by Falcon Oast Graphic Art
Printed by Cox & Wyman Ltd, Reading, Berks

2 4 6 8 10 9 7 5 3 1

1

"Hey, Leo!" one of his classmates shouted as a group of them headed for the school gates. "Five-a-side at the Rec – you coming?"

Leo Banks shook his head. "Nah. Can't."

As he turned away there was a burst of laughter behind him, then someone called, "What's the matter – babysitting again?"

"Leo's a wimp!"

"Yeah! He *always* does what Mummy and Daddy tell him!"

Leo felt his face reddening, then he reminded himself that it didn't matter. It was a straight choice, anyway: no babysitting, no

Internet. And there wasn't anything he could do about it.

Someone came hurrying up behind him, and a voice at his elbow said, "Ignore 'em, I would. They're a load of dummies. Like my dad says, 'Rise above it'."

Mikey Morris was jogging along beside him. Mikey only came up to Leo's shoulder, but the fact that he was the smallest kid in their year didn't bother him. The only thing that *ever* bothered Mikey was not being able to solve a maths problem. He was the class brainbox, and his two big obsessions were computers and outer space. Where everyone else's ambition was to play for United or something like that, Mikey's was to crack the secret of faster-than-light travel. Their class teacher reckoned that he'd end up either a famous batty professor, or just plain batty. He even looked the part, with his spiky black hair and round, blue-rimmed glasses.

Leo laughed. "I don't care, really," he said. "I can play football any time."

"If you're into football." Mikey wasn't, of course. "So you get some time on your dad's modem tonight, then?" Mikey was one of the few who knew about the arrangement.

"Yeah. There's this new game I heard about,

called 'Intergalactica' – you can download it, and—"

"Tried it," Mikey interrupted. "Don't bother; it's little-kid stuff. Hey, look – if you want something *really* great, I found a new website last night. It's got all the latest NASA stuff on it, and there's this article by the Head of Space Technology at—"

"Forget it!" Leo held up his hands before Mikey could say any more. "I said *games*, not brains!"

Mikey shrugged, pulling a face. "Oh, well. If you're just another dumbo Net-surfer, I s'pose you can't help it." He grinned mischievously to show he was only joking. Or sort of. "Have fun, then. See you tomorrow."

"Yeah," said Leo, grinning back. "See you."

The trouble was, Leo's mum and dad didn't trust him to have his own phone connection to the Internet. Leo didn't think that was very fair. He'd only run up a huge bill once, and he'd said he was sorry and he'd never do it again, but Dad was immovable. He'd taken Leo's modem away, and no modem, of course, meant no Internet. Instead, Leo had been offered a deal. He could borrow and use Dad's modem – but only when he babysat Thomas and Tina, his kid brother and sister. It was hard to imagine anything more horrendous than looking after twin toddlers, but Leo hadn't had much choice. So now, whenever Mum and Dad went out, he got his chance to go on the Internet.

Actually, as little kids went, Thomas and Tina could have been a lot worse. They were just getting to the age when some of what they said made sense, which meant that when Leo told them NO, they knew what he meant. They didn't take much notice, but at least they knew. And once he got them to sleep (which, admittedly, took some doing), they usually stayed put.

So by the time he got home, Leo had forgotten about his classmates' teasing and was feeling pretty cheerful. He'd made a new friend on the Net – a boy called Scott who lived in Colorado, USA. With any luck, there'd be a message waiting. Then – ignoring Mikey – he could check out that new Intergalactica game.

His parents were almost ready to go out. They were both academics (Leo found that a bit embarrassing, but he'd learned to live with it) and were always going off to talks and lectures. Tonight's was something about modern art, and Leo pretended to be interested as Mum enthused about it while they waited for Dad to come downstairs. When he appeared, Mum stopped in the middle of her sentence. She waved vaguely at the fridge, said there was "something" in there for tea, then with a wave and an even vaguer "Be good!" she wafted out of the door in Dad's wake.

Vague was a pretty good word to describe Mum. Dad too – at least when he wasn't grumbling about the phone bill. Leo listened as the car drove erratically away, then stuck his head in the fridge to see what he could eat. Microwave pasta. That was OK, providing there was a tasty sauce to go with it.

There was, so he shoved what the packets called "three generous servings" into the microwave and waited for it to ping. Thomas and Tina were in the sitting-room. He knew, because he could hear their favourite Disney video blaring from the TV. The twins had two big fixations in their lives right now: Disney movies and nursery rhymes. One nursery rhyme in particular. *Incy Wincy Spider*. Leo thought about it, and cringed. How many times would he have to recite it tonight? Unless they got bored with it pretty soon, he'd be doing that blasted rhyme in his sleep!

He was in the middle of his food when the video ended. About ten seconds later there was a thunder of feet and two voices yelled his name, or a version of it.

"Lee-bo, *Leee-bo*!"

"Come 'n' play, Leebo!"

"Want to play! IncyWincyPider!" They hadn't got the hang of saying "spider" yet.

"Yeah! Incy Wincy, Incy-Wincy-Pincy-poo-poo!" And a rude noise to go with it. The twins piled into the kitchen and started jumping about by Leo's chair.

"All right, all right!" Leo groaned, grabbing his glass of Coke before they could knock it flying. "Just let me eat, willya?"

"Leebo eat his tea," said Tina. "I had mine!"

"And me," Thomas agreed. "IncyWincy-Pider! *Now!*"

Reason wasn't going to work, Leo knew. Oh, well. He could re-heat the rest of his pasta later. And the sooner he got this over, the sooner they'd wear themselves out and go to sleep.

"Come on then, you pair of monsters!" He got up, ignoring Tina, who'd suddenly decided she was a tiger and was trying to bite his leg. "Up the stairs, and let's play!"

* * *

Incy Wincy Spider, climbing up the spout;
Down came the rain, and washed the spider out!
Out came the sun, and dried up all the rain;
So Incy Wincy Spider climbed up the spout again. . .

"Oh, shut up!" Leo said aloud to himself. That wretched rhyme was going round and round in his head. At this rate, it'd haunt him for the rest of his life!

He wriggled out from under his desk, where he'd been plugging Dad's modem into his computer. Everything ready. Right, then. Now for some sanity!

It had taken eight "Incy Wincy Spiders", with finger-wiggling accompaniment, before the twins had had enough. At last, though, they'd gone to bed, and Leo had fingers and toes crossed that they would go to sleep and not start bouncing around and yelling for stories or drinks of water. Pity you couldn't keep tiny tots in cages, he thought with a grin.

He switched his computer on, and while it bleeped and chuntered through its start-up routine, he stared out of the window. It looked as if it was going to rain. Hard enough to wash

Incy Wincy lousy Spider right down the spout and half way across the garden, with any luck! The sky was a grim purplish-black, and there was an ominous feeling in the air. Could be a storm. He'd better watch out; storms could damage computers, so if one *did* start, he should be ready to switch off quickly.

But the storm didn't break – at least, not for a while. Leo collected his e-mail (there was one from Scott, which he printed out to read later in case he did have to switch off), then searched for the Intergalactica game.

He couldn't find it, but he did find something else. It was a website for a new game that you could download on to your own computer and play. It was free, and it looked like fun. There was only one off-putting thing about it.

It was called "INCY WINCY SPIDER".

"I don't believe it!" Leo groaned, smacking a hand against his forehead. Then suddenly he got the giggles. *OK, OK*, he thought. *I give in!* If the nursery rhyme *was* going to haunt him, he might as well make the most of it. He'd be a prat if he passed up the chance to get a great game for nothing, just because he didn't like its title! Now: where were the on-screen instructions for loading it?

The computer whirred and beeped and

chugged as the game came down the phone line. It took quite a long time to load it all, but at last the screen showed a message reading, *All done! Now you can start exploring Incy Wincy's web! Just click GO.*

Leo clicked GO.

For a few seconds, nothing happened.

Then two things happened.

The first thing was that the picture on Leo's computer changed to a spider's web that covered the whole screen. In the middle of it was a completely demented cartoon spider, with eyes like two fried eggs and rows of gnashing teeth. The spider bounced up and down, and the web shook madly, making Leo feel dizzy. Music started to blare out of the speakers.

A split second later, came the other thing.

It was a gargantuan flash that turned the whole room electric blue. And it was accompanied by a crash of thunder that roared and boomed overhead like a bomb going off.

There was an awful noise from Leo's computer, almost drowned by the thunder.

Then all the electricity in the house went *phut*.

2

The amazing thing was, the twins hadn't even stirred.

Leo had expected them to start screaming in terror, but the thunderbolt hadn't woken them, and they slept happily on while he groped in the cupboard under the stairs, trying to find the fuse box.

Luckily, the house's electric circuits hadn't been blown. All that had happened was that a surge had tripped the safety cut-out. When Leo found the switch and pushed it down, the lights came on again.

So did his computer. When he got back to his bedroom (after checking on Thomas and Tina), it was going through its start-up routine. Leo hoped nothing had been damaged, especially not Dad's modem. If *that* was bust, he'd be in trouble up to his ears!

He breathed a sigh of relief when it seemed that everything was all right. All his programs were there. The speakers were working. He'd even managed to get that new game. . .

Hang on a minute. The new game. He hadn't clicked on GO again, so why was there a demented-looking spider, with fried-egg eyes and a lot of teeth, stomping across his screen?

Then the music started. It was obviously supposed to be spooky, but it wouldn't have scared a hamster. Leo ground his teeth together as he realized you could sing *Incy Wincy Spider* to it, and clicked his mouse button frantically, trying to make it stop.

It didn't stop. And neither did the spider, which had now stomped half way across the screen. It was also twice as big as it had been a minute ago. Its eyes rolled and it was positively *leering* at him.

Then the first strands of the web appeared, snaking out from where the spider crouched, and started to spread. There were dozens of them. No – there were *hundreds*! Leo's jaw dropped open in alarm as he began to realize what was happening.

Slowly, bit by bit, everything on his screen

was disappearing. Everything, that is, except the strands of the spider's web. They were all knitting together, blotting out whatever was behind them. Half Leo's program icons had vanished already. The rest would be gone in another minute or two. And in the middle of the chaos, the cartoon spider bounced gleefully up and down, gnashing its teeth, as mad, tinny laughter rang out from the speakers.

Leo tried everything he could think of. He clicked buttons, thumped keys, pleaded, shouted – but nothing made any difference. The web went on spreading. The spider went on bouncing and gnashing and cackling. And at last there was only one hope.

He switched the whole machine off.

For an awful moment he thought that even that wouldn't work. The spider seemed to stay on the screen for ages, still leering at him and waggling four of its legs defiantly.

Then suddenly, blessedly, everything shut down.

Leo stared at his computer. Outside, the sky was still ominous and murky, and thunder was grumbling in the distance. Had the storm done this? Leo wondered. Had that electrical surge somehow glitched the computer and made the new game go wrong on him? Or was there another explanation? Maybe he ought to switch on again, see what happened.

As he leaned forward, reaching for the power button, something caught his eye. It was the e-mail from Scott in Colorado; the one he'd printed out but hadn't read yet.

Three words stood out. They were: *INCY WINCY SPIDER*.

Leo goggled. This was just too crazy to be a coincidence! Snatching up the page, he started to read what Scott had to say.

And realized what he'd gone and done.

Hi, Leo, Scott's message began. *Thought I better tell you about a problem virus that's going round. It makes out it's a free game called "Incy Wincy Spider", but if you download it, you REALLY got trouble! A coupla kids in school picked it up, and boy, did it screw their computers! What happens is. . .*

Leo didn't need Scott to tell him what happened. He already knew. What on earth was he going to do *now*? If only he'd read the e-mail first! But he hadn't, and though he knew how to use computers, he didn't know the first thing about programming or de-bugging or whatever they called it when you had to sort out trouble. He didn't even know where to start!

But then his spirits lifted, as he remembered someone who *did* know.

He swapped the modem over for an ordinary phone, looked up a number, and dialled.

"Oh, hi, Mrs Morris," he said when it was answered at the other end. "It's Leo Banks here. . . Yeah, fine, thanks. . . They're fine, too. . . And the twins, yeah. . . Um . . . could I speak to Mikey, please?"

"Hoo-wee! Have you got a problem!" Mikey finished reading Scott's message, then turned his attention to the computer. "I've heard of this Incy Wincy virus. It's a real nightmare."

"Thanks a bunch!" Leo groaned. "The thing is, can you fix it?"

"Dunno. I can *try*. But I can't promise anything. And Dad says I've got to be home before it gets dark."

Mikey lived near by and it had only taken him ten minutes to get to Leo's on his bike. The evenings stayed light now that it was May, so Leo figured that they'd have about an hour and a half. He hoped and prayed Mikey could do it in that time.

"OK." Mikey plonked himself down on Leo's chair and wiggled his fingers over the computer keyboard like a pianist getting ready to play. "First things first. Let's switch on and see what happens."

Leo crossed his fingers *and* his toes as they waited for the computer to start up. *Chunter . . . chunter . . . rattle-rattle-BLEEP!* All the familiar noises. It looked as if everything was going to be fine. . .

Until an awful cackling came over the speakers, and in the middle of the screen appeared—

"Oh, no!" Leo yelped. "It's still there!"

It certainly was, bouncing and leering and gnashing, as the web exploded outwards around it. Mikey said, "Uh-oh!" and dived for the OFF button, and in the moment before the screen went dark, it seemed to Leo that the spider looked furious.

Mikey whistled and sat back. "That was close!"

"It's bad?" Leo asked.

Mikey nodded. "It's bad. The virus has got right into your system, and it's going to take some getting out. But I *think* I can do it."

"If you can," said Leo with feeling, "then I owe you the hugest favour ever! Anything you want!"

"Careful!" Mikey grinned. "I might take you up on that. Now." He crouched forward again, and his eyes gleamed with the light of battle. "I've brought my anti-virus disks. So let's see how clever Incy Wincy *really* is. . ."

It took over an hour, but Mikey did it. To Leo, watching, it was awesome. Mikey was like some brilliant super-android out of an SF movie. His fingers flew over the mouse and keyboard, he slammed disks in and out at boggling speed – Leo half expected to see sparks coming out of his ears as his brain overloaded.

And, bit by bit, the web that blotted out Leo's screen started to break apart.

The spider was the last thing to go. Mikey froze it in mid-movement, four legs raised menacingly and the other four curled under its bulgy body. Then, *click . . . click-click . . . BLEEEP!* And the spider vanished.

"Whooo!" Mikey puffed out his cheeks as if he was blowing up a balloon. But he looked very pleased. "Done it! Incy Wincy Spider's gone, and unless you do something dumb again, he won't be back."

Leo was so busy admiring Mikey that he didn't notice the insult. "Thanks!" he said earnestly. "That was *brilliant*!"

Mikey shrugged. "It's easy really, when you know how. You could learn to do it." He looked at Leo sideways. "Well, perhaps not. . ." Then he grinned. "Hey, how about a glass of Coke? I'm thirsty!"

They were drinking their Cokes and watching Leo's computer (just in case, Mikey said), when there was a rumpus along the landing, and Thomas came piling into the room with Tina at his heels.

"Leebo, Leebo! We got up!" Then they stopped as they saw Mikey.

"Who that?" Tina demanded.

Mikey raised his eyebrows at them. "Hi," he said. "I'm Mikey."

The twins stared at him. Then Thomas said, "You got glasses. You look silly."

Tina nodded agreement. "Yeah. Silly." She beamed at Mikey. "Can you do IncyWincy-Pider?"

Mikey nearly spluttered Coke all over the floor, but he calmed down when Leo explained. They both did Incy Wincy Spider for the twins, just once, then Mikey said he'd better go, or he'd be skinned alive for being late.

Leo waved from the window as Mikey biked away. The rain had stopped now and the sky was clearing. Mum and Dad should be back soon; they'd said they wouldn't be late. Thomas and Tina were pestering for a story. And the last thing Leo wanted to think about right now was computers.

He switched his machine off with a sigh of relief. The twins were in their beds and had promised to stay there till he came to read to them. So he left his room, flicking the light out as he went.

The empty room grew gloomier and gloomier as dusk fell. Soon it was almost dark. From the twins' bedroom came the drone of Leo's voice reading, and occasional shouts or giggles. Otherwise, the house was quiet.

No one was there to watch the computer. No one saw the screen start to glow with a strange greeny-blue light. It shouldn't have been possible. The computer was switched off. But it happened. And at the heart of the glow was a single black dot. The dot expanded till it was about the size of an egg. Then suddenly it, and the eerie glow, vanished.

Half a minute later, there was a tiny little scratching, scrabbling noise. And from the back of the machine, a *thing* emerged. It was very small. It didn't have much of a shape.

But it did have a lot of legs. . .

Another sound whispered through the room; a sort of *pitterpatter, pitterpatter*, as if something was scuttling very fast and furtively. The small, shapeless something skittered across the top of Leo's desk, then slid down one of the desk legs to the floor. It darted into the darkest corner, where no one ever looked.

And it started to spin itself a teeny, *teeny* web.

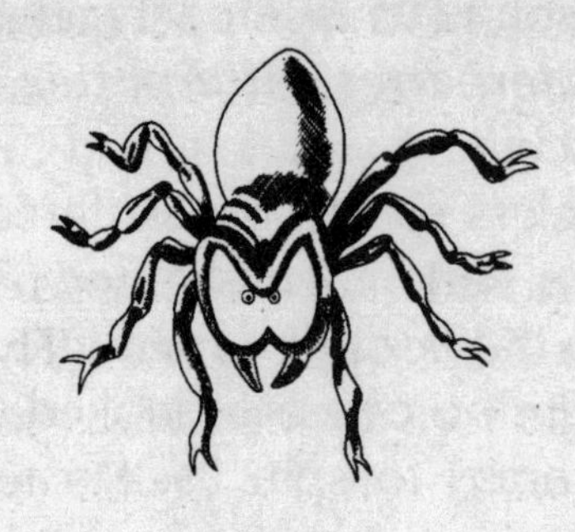

3

Two days later, Leo was babysitting again. And he got another e-mail from Scott.

Hi, Leo, it began. *Got your last e-mail. I'm real glad to know you fixed the problem with that virus. Your friend Mikey sounds cool – I could use him in math lessons!*

I tried to find out where that booby-trapped game came from, but no luck. Tracking it back's like tangling in the biggest spider web you ever saw! But I mailed some official people and told them what's going on, so maybe they'll get whoever started it. If you and Mikey turn anything up, let me know. Otherwise, just don't go downloading any more dodgy freebies, OK? See you – Scott.

Smiling, Leo closed the computer's mailbox. He'd reply to Scott next time. There was homework to do tonight, as well as something he wanted to watch on TV, so he could only spend a little while on the Net. Long enough to check out a couple of the websites he was interested in and see if there was anything new on them.

He'd just got nicely started when he heard a noise from the twins' room next door.

It wasn't quite a song, but it had a definite rhythm, sort of: *dumty, dumty, dum-dum; dumty, dumty DUM*. Leo thought there were words, but he couldn't make them out.

Then it clicked.

"I don't *believe* it. . ." His heart sank into his trainers. Not *again*! With a sigh, he got up and plodded to the twins' room.

Thomas and Tina were awake all right. Opening the door, Leo could see them by the glow of their nightlight. They were both sitting up in bed. And now he *could* hear the words of their chant.

"Incy Wincy Pider, climbing up the POUT!

Down camed the rain, and washed the pider OUT!" Thomas was doing the hand movements, and Tina was giggling.

"OK, you two!" Leo called. The chant stopped, and the twins stared at him.

"'Lo, Leebo," said Tina.

"I'll give you 'hallo Leebo'!" Leo growled. "You're supposed to be asleep!"

"Don't want to," said Thomas. "Not sleepy."

"We're *playing*," Tina added. "IncyWincy-Pider." She waggled her fingers menacingly at Leo and pulled a face.

"Well, I've got better things to do!" Leo snapped. "I'm *not* doing Incy Wincy Spider again, get it?"

They looked at him blankly, and to his surprise Thomas said, "Don't care. *We're* playing it, not you!"

"Yeah, not you," Tina agreed. "*Our* game. Go 'way!"

They turned their backs on him and started the chant again. "Incy Wincy Pider, climbing up the POUT!"

Leo was astonished. They'd never done this before. They *always* pestered him to do the rhyme for them. Now, suddenly, they weren't the least bit interested in him.

Well, what the heck? he thought. No harm

was going to come to Thomas and Tina in their own bedroom. So long as he got them to sleep before Mum and Dad came back, he might as well leave them to it, and grab the chance for some peace and quiet!

"Night night, then," he said.

The twins ignored him and went on chanting.

Leo turned and started to walk out of the room.

Then, as he reached the doorway, he flinched.

Something had *touched* him. He'd felt it quite definitely, on his face and chest. It was as if there was a piece of elastic stretched across the doorway and he'd walked straight into it.

Leo stared at the space in front of him. He couldn't see anything. Then he reached out and waved his hand around in the doorway. Nothing at all: just empty air.

Uh? he thought. Cautiously, he stepped forward – and walked through the door without feeling anything. Out on the landing, he stopped and looked back into the bedroom. He must have imagined the strange feeling. Either that, or he was going crackers.

The twins were engrossed in their game again and took no notice of him. Leo shook his head, baffled, then shut the door and went back to his own room. Slumping down on the chair in front of his desk, he reached for the computer mouse.

"What the—"

It scuttled off the screen so fast that he only got the briefest glimpse. But that was enough. The cartoon spider, with its fried-egg eyes and gnashing teeth, was back!

"Oh, no!" Leo clapped both hands to his skull. "Mikey, you idiot! You told me you'd got rid of it!"

Feverishly, he started to call up files, looking for the spider – or, worse, for signs of damage to his system. He didn't find either. But that didn't prove anything. He needed help again, and fast, so hastily he plugged in the phone.

Luckily, Mikey was at home. But when Leo started to chew him out for not getting rid of the virus, he interrupted indignantly.

"Hey, wait a minute! Who says I didn't get rid of it?"

Leo told him what had just happened. "It zoomed off the screen when I came back, and when I looked in the files the way you showed me, I couldn't find it. But it was *there*."

"It can't have been!" said Mikey firmly.

"You're seeing things, Leo, mate. Got spiders on the brain, if you ask me!"

Leo felt annoyed, probably because Mikey's remark was too close to the truth. "Don't be a prat!" he snapped. "I do *not* go around seeing things that aren't there! You told me it had gone, it hasn't, so I want to know what I'm supposed to do about it!"

A heavy, long-suffering sigh came down the phone. "OK, OK; keep your brain in one piece! Are you by your computer? Right. Well, this is what you do. . ."

They didn't find what they were looking for. Leo followed all Mikey's complicated instructions, but after the best part of an hour there was no sign of the spider anywhere in the system.

"Right," Mikey said at last. "We've tried positively, definitely and absolutely everything. It's not there, Leo. You *were* seeing things."

Leo couldn't argue. Despite what he'd said earlier, he trusted Mikey to know what he was doing. If he said the virus was gone, then it was gone – end of story.

But what *had* he seen scurrying off the screen. . .?

"You'd better get off the phone," Mikey added, "or your mum and dad'll go ballistic when they see the bill."

Leo gulped as he realized how long they'd been talking. "Yeah, right," he said. "But Mikey, what if—"

"Look, leave it, will you? If there *is* a 'what if', we can't do anything about it now! Keep an eye on your computer, and we'll talk at school tomorrow, OK?"

"OK," Leo agreed reluctantly. "See you then. And . . . thanks."

"Thought you'd never get round to mentioning it!" said Mikey. "See you."

When he'd put the phone down, Leo sat staring at his computer for some time. It all looked perfectly normal. There was no scuttling flicker in the corner of the screen, and – more importantly – no sign of the spider's web starting to sprawl over the picture. Maybe Mikey was right. Maybe he *had* been seeing things. It was the only explanation that made any sense.

There wasn't a sound from the twins' room now, so they must have gone to sleep at last. All the same, Leo thought he'd better check, so he tiptoed along the landing.

As he opened the door he remembered the weird feeling he'd had earlier that something had touched him. Suddenly he didn't want to go through the door, in case it happened again.

Idiot! he told himself. All the same, his teeth were clenched as he stepped forward. . .

It didn't happen again. And Thomas and Tina were fast asleep. They'd swapped beds, and Tina was almost invisible under about half a tonne of toys, including Thomas's giant-size teddy. But that was perfectly normal. Everything was perfectly normal. Nothing to worry about at all.

Leo backed out, closing the door very quietly. He felt jittery, and he didn't know why, and he didn't like it. When he went into his own bedroom again the feeling got worse. He fought it, telling himself he was acting like a wimp. But he didn't want to stay upstairs. The computer screen seemed to be *staring*, as if there was something alive in there, watching him. He wanted to switch it off.

Wimpy or not, Leo gave in to the jitters. He breathed out in relief as the computer went off with a descending whine and the screen blanked. Nearly time for that TV programme. He'd watch in it the sitting-room instead of up here.

He didn't turn his bedroom light out. In fact, as he hurried downstairs, he pressed every light switch there was, until the whole house was blazing brilliantly. Mum would be annoyed, but he'd just say he forgot to turn them off. Whatever happened, he wasn't going to own up to the real reason.

After twenty minutes Leo was feeling better. He was slumped in an armchair, absorbed in the TV. And every light in the room was ablaze. He didn't hear the car pull up, and didn't hear a key turn in the front door.

He only realized that his parents were home when he heard Mum scream.

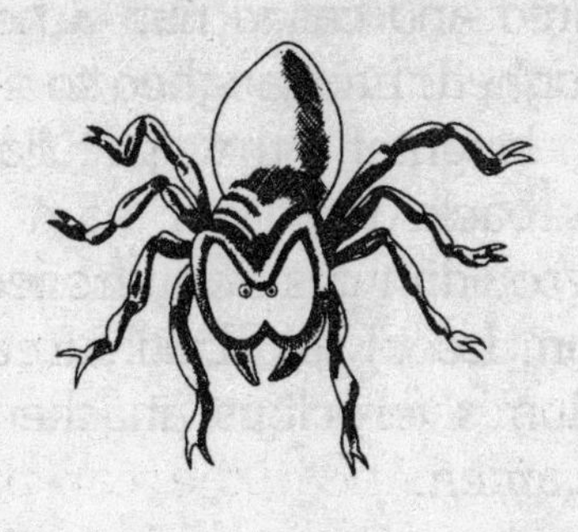

4

"I couldn't help it!" Mum said. Her voice was still shaky. "It scuttled across the floor right in front of me, and it was *enormous*!" She looked apologetically at Dad and Leo. "You know how I hate them!"

Mum had always been terrified of spiders. Even a tiny one was enough to make her squeal and run away. As for the one she'd just seen. . .

"It was – it was—" Mum held her hands apart as though measuring, spreading them wider and wider.

"Must've been all of seven centimetres across," said Dad drily, "including legs."

Mum glared and called him a heartless pig, and Dad laughed. Leo laughed too. But underneath the laughter, the peculiar, squirmy feeling was back. However hard he tried, it seemed he couldn't get away from spiders.

"Come on, Leo," said Dad. "Let's see if we can find Mum's ferocious attacker and put it out in the garden."

Mum glared again and said huffily that she was going to check on the twins. She stomped upstairs, and Leo and Dad spent the next few minutes crawling around on the hall floor. But the spider knew better than to hang around; it had hidden itself thoroughly.

"Oh, well." Dad straightened up at last. "Unless the spider's stone deaf, that scream was probably enough to make sure it never comes back! What Mum doesn't see can't hurt her, eh? Right; I'm going to check a few things in my study. Have you put the modem back?"

Leo flushed guiltily. "Oh, er . . . I forgot."

"Well, go upstairs and *un*-forget!" Dad headed for his study door. "Go on, hurry up!"

Leo looked at the staircase. This was crazy – there was no reason why he shouldn't go up there. The computer was off. There was nothing lurking inside it that was going to jump out and bite him.

"Leo!" Dad snapped.

"Uh – yeah. I'm going. Sorry, Dad."

He sprinted up the stairs as fast as any spider could scurry.

Try as he might, Leo couldn't get to sleep that night. He read until Mum came up and told him to turn his light off or else, then lay listening to the sounds of his parents getting ready for bed. Even when the house was totally quiet, he still couldn't doze off. He kept raising his head to look across the room at the computer screen. All he could make out in the dark was a faintly shining reflection. And, of course, there was nothing to see anyway; the screen was switched off. But he *couldn't* get rid of the fear that, next time he looked, he'd see it light up, and that mad cartoon spider would appear.

At last he got so wound up that he had to do something. Switching his lamp on, he scrambled out of bed, took his school jacket from the cupboard and hung it over the screen. Right! If anything happened now, he wouldn't see it. The spider could turn up and do a break-dancing display for all he cared. He didn't want to know.

He got back into bed and turned the lamp

off again. That was better. Now, maybe, he could shut his eyes and—

The thought jolted to a halt as, from somewhere not far away, he heard a noise.

Scritch. Scritch.

Leo sat bolt upright. It was only a tiny sound, but it was coming from the wall to his left.

Scritch. A pause. Then: *scrabble-scrabble-scrabble!*

Leo's skin crawled. The noise seemed to be inside the wall, and very low down. What on earth *was* it?

Then suddenly, muffled but unmistakable, he heard a giggle.

Leo could have kicked himself. What an idiot he was! The twins' room was on the other side of the wall, and that giggle had sounded *exactly* like Tina.

So they were awake again, were they? Scratching on the wall, trying to wake him up. Yeah, *very* funny. Well, he wasn't going to take the bait. If Thomas and Tina wanted to mess around, then Mum or Dad could sort it out. It wasn't his problem.

Leo flopped back on the pillow. He shut his eyes. And when the mumbled chant of "*Incy Wincy Pider, climbing up the POUT!*" started to come through the wall, he ignored it.

* * *

At break next morning, Mikey came looking for Leo.

"Any more trouble?" he asked.

Leo shook his head. He'd just about managed to convince himself that he hadn't really seen the spider at all. Or at least, if he had, then Mikey's instructions last night had finally got rid of it.

"Told you there wouldn't be, didn't I?" Mikey sounded smug. "Mind you, it *was* a bit weird. I mean – well, I know what I said, but you're not the sort who goes seeing things. So I've been wondering. . ."

"Wondering what?" said Leo.

"That American mate of yours, the one who first heard about the virus. I just wondered if he's found out anything else."

"Scott?" Leo shrugged. "He hadn't last I heard. But I'll give you his e-mail address if you want. He won't mind, and then you can ask him yourself."

Mikey brightened. "Great! You see, I've got this idea for inventing a new program that'd let people track these things back to whoever started them. So Scott could be useful."

Leo grinned. Mikey talked about inventing new programs as if it was as easy as blinking. But then, to him, it probably was.

"OK," he said. "I'll write the address down and give it to you at lunchtime."

The end-of-break bell rang then, and there wasn't time to talk any more. Leo's class had Art for the rest of the morning, and to his dismay he discovered that he'd left all his drawing things *and* his half-finished project at home. Ms Porter wasn't the sort of teacher you could make excuses to, and he flushed red as she hauled him over the carpet.

"It wouldn't matter so much if you weren't any good at Art, Leo," she said crossly, "but you are – and I thought you liked it!"

"I do, Ms Porter!" Leo protested. "It was just that . . . there were things going on last night, and I forgot."

"What sort of things?" Ms Porter demanded.

Before Leo could answer, Mikey, who was next to him, piped up helpfully, "He's been having trouble with his computer, Ms Porter. I know, 'cause he phoned me for help last night. There's this virus going round, you see, and—"

The teacher silenced him with a glare. "Thank you, Mikey," she said icily. "I get the idea. And I suppose it's asking *too* much to put school work before your computer games!"

Mikey started to say indignantly, "*I* don't play games, I—" but Leo dug him hard in the ribs. "*Drop me in it again, why don't you?*" Leo hissed.

"*Sorry*," Mikey whispered. "*I was only trying to help*."

"*Well, don't!*" Ms Porter was starting to look dangerous, so both boys shut up. As Leo couldn't get on with his project, he was told do borrow some materials and do something else – no, Ms Porter didn't care what it was; just *something*. So he scrounged a pencil from Mikey (this was partly his fault, after all) and started to draw.

It was only a doodle, really. He didn't think about it properly, he just let his mind wander while the pencil did what it wanted. After a while, Ms Porter came and looked over his shoulder. Then she bent closer.

"Interesting," she said. "You've got the start of a good design there, Leo."

Surprised, Leo blinked, and looked at his drawing properly for the first time.

It was a picture of a spider's web. Very neat and very regular, it spread out from the middle of the page like a mosaic pattern. Leo was boggled. He didn't even know he'd been doing that. It had just sort of happened, all by itself.

And right at the centre of the pattern was a spider. Its body was filled in, making a solid black blob. All except for two goggling eyes.

Ms Porter was looking very pleased. "I think you ought to continue with this," she told him. "You could add some colour, maybe *here*, and *here*," jabbing with a finger. "It would be great for a tile, or a window, or. . ."

She went on, but Leo wasn't listening. Instead, he was thinking, *Incy Wincy Spider . . . I can't get away from it!*

The teacher's voice swelled back again, like a radio being turned up, ". . . till you've finished your main project, then look at it again. All right?"

"Er . . . yeah," said Leo. "Right. Yeah."

"Good. I'll put it in the art cupboard at the end of the lesson. That way, you won't forget it, will you?"

Leo grinned weakly. To tell the truth, he didn't want the picture put in the art cupboard. He wanted to tear it up, drop the bits in a bucket and set fire to them. He did not want this picture to *exist*.

And he didn't know why.

Leo was scratchy and jumpy for the rest of that day. He forgot to give Mikey Scott's e-mail address, and he couldn't concentrate properly on lessons. He was glad when school finished.

Mikey called after him at the gates, and reminded him about Scott.

"Oh – oh, right," Leo said. "Sorry." He repeated the address and Mikey wrote it on the back of one hand. Then, as Leo was about to walk away, he said, "You all right, Leo?"

Leo stopped. "Me? Yeah, course I am. Why?"

"You've been ratty all afternoon. And that picture you did in Art. . ."

"What about it?"

Mikey recoiled. "OK, no need to bite my ears off! I thought it was a bit weird, that's all. Why the spider's web?"

Leo shrugged. "I dunno. I drew it, that's all."

"Mmm," said Mikey, which could have meant anything. Then: "You *sure* you haven't had any more trouble with the computer?"

"No," Leo told him.

"Oh. Right. I just wondered."

He hurried off, leaving Leo staring after him.

The first thing Leo heard when he got home and opened the front door was a mad din from the sitting-room. The twins were in there.

They'd invented a new game that seemed to involve climbing over the furniture and screaming a lot, and Mum had given up and left them to it while she messed around in the garden.

The moment Thomas and Tina saw Leo, they pounced.

"Leebo, Leebo!"

"Come 'n' play our game!"

"Yeah! BANG! YEEZOW! Leebo dead!"

"No way!" The twins had got hold of his arms and were trying to pull them out of their sockets; Leo wrenched himself free and backed away.

"C'mon, Leebo!" Tina wheedled. "*Pleease!*"

"*No*. I'm too busy – *oww*! Let *go*!"

"Pullhisarmsandlegsoff!" Thomas shouted gleefully. Tina whooped – then suddenly her expression grew sly.

"'Nother game, then," she said. "*I* know . . . *INCYWINCYPIDER*! Incy Wincy, Incy Wincy!"

They both began to bounce round him, chanting "Incy Wincy!" at the tops of their voices. With a yell, Leo broke away from them, turned round and ran upstairs. The twins came charging after him, but they weren't as fast as he was, so they'd hardly started by the time he reached the safety of his room.

He rushed in, slammed the door behind him, swung round—

And felt as if the floor had dropped away under his feet.

There was his familiar bedroom. The bed. The cupboard. The desk. The chair. The computer. It was all exactly as it usually was.

Except that *everything* was covered with spider's webs.

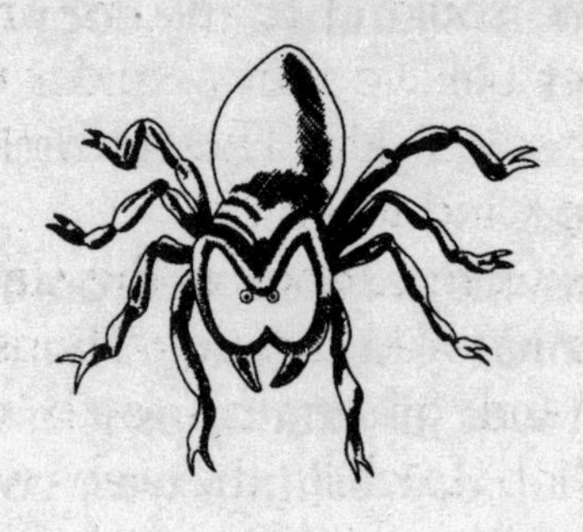

5

It was totally *crazy*. When Leo had left for school this morning, his bedroom had been perfectly all right. Now, just a few hours later, *this*.

The room looked like a set from a Haunted House movie. All it needed was a couple of bats flying around and it would have been perfect. And if Mum was to set eyes on it. . .

Leo tore downstairs, jumping over Thomas and Tina who were half way up. In the kitchen he grabbed rubber gloves and a dustpan and brush, then steeled himself to brave the bedroom again. He didn't want to touch those cobwebs. He didn't want to go anywhere near them. But he couldn't tell Mum, or even Dad. They'd never believe that a spider could make all this mess so quickly. They'd think he'd done it himself, to wind Mum up.

The twins were sitting on the stairs, looking baffled. Leo ignored their questions, tore past them again and, gritting his teeth, went to get on with the job. Luckily, the webs were easy to clear away, and he'd got rid of nearly half of them when he was interrupted by two familiar voices.

"What you doing, Leebo?"

"Poo! Look! Dirty stuff all *over* the place!"

The twins had appeared at the door, which Leo had forgotten to shut behind him. They ran in and started poking their fingers into the cobwebs. Then Tina grabbed a handful and wiped them in Thomas's hair.

"Out of here! Go on, *scoot*!" Leo yelled.

They ignored him. Thomas was on his hands and knees now, crawling round the floor. "Lots of piders!" he announced. "IncyWincy, Incy-Wincy, Incy—"

Leo didn't bother to argue. He just grabbed them both, one after the other, and dumped them outside on the landing, slamming the door in their faces before they could dart back in.

He leaned against the door and shut his eyes. His heart was doing somersaults. Outside there was ominous silence for a few moments, but then he heard small feet thudding away. Letting his breath out in an enormous sigh, Leo opened his eyes again and got back to his task. After emptying the dustpan eight times out of the window, there were still traces of cobwebs here and there. Down below, he could see Mum still in the garden, but she hadn't noticed him. So long as she didn't decide to come back indoors just as he was tipping the pan again, and get a faceful. . .

He was finishing the last corners when something made him pause. A noise. He'd heard that noise before. Last night. A scratching and scrabbling, that sounded for a moment as if it was coming from inside the wall.

Only it wasn't, of course. Leo knew perfectly well where it was coming from, and he growled inwardly. Those kids were at it again! Well, to heck with it – they could carry on till they were blue in the face for all he cared. He wasn't going to take any notice!

He switched the radio on, to let Thomas and Tina know that he wasn't going to play their game, and carried on sweeping up. The loud music didn't put the twins off, though. And, annoyingly, it didn't completely drown the scratching noises. Leo could still hear them: *scritch-scritch, scrabble-scrabble*, and it got on his nerves. Then, as he was taking the very last panful to the window, Mum opened the bedroom door, making him jump with surprise.

"Leo! Turn that radio down – they'll hear you half way up the street!" she shouted.

Leo turned it down. "Sorry, Mum," he said. The scratching noises had stopped, anyway; the twins must have heard Mum coming.

Mum stared at the newly brushed room and asked, "Whatever are you doing?"

"Oh . . . just clearing up a bit. You know."

She blinked, astonished. "I can't remember when you last tidied your room without being told to! Are you feeling all right?" Then her expression changed. "Or are you trying to get into my good books because you've done something awful?"

"Course not!" said Leo indignantly. "I just thought I'd do it, that's all."

"Hmm," said Mum suspiciously. "I suppose I'll find out the truth sooner or later, won't I? Well, if you're feeling so helpful, there's something else you can do for me."

"Oh?" Leo said warily. "What?"

"I want to go into the garden shed, but I

can't, because there's a *huge* spider's web across the door." Mum shuddered. "Go and get rid of it for me, will you?"

Leo's jaw dropped. *Another* one? But then he reminded himself that there wasn't anything weird about that. Spiders were always making webs in the garden. The garden was the proper place for spiders' webs.

Unlike bedrooms.

He shut his mouth again and swallowed. "OK," he said, in what he hoped was his normal voice. "I've – um – got the brush here; I'll use that."

There was nothing strange about the web in the garden, and there was just an ordinary spider in the middle of it. Mum watched while Leo put the spider on a plant and brushed the web into the pan.

"There are spiders everywhere these last few days," she said. "I've never *seen* so many out here! You expect it in the autumn, but not at this time of year. Thanks, Leo. That'll do fine; I can go in there now."

She vanished into the shed, leaving Leo standing on the path and thinking about what she'd just said. *Spiders everywhere these last few days*. Were there? He hadn't noticed. But then he hardly ever went into the garden.

So if Mum was right, where were they all coming from?

What was going *on*?

He put the brush and pan away and went to check on his room. He knew that the webs wouldn't have reappeared – they couldn't possibly have done in the space of a few minutes. But all the same he could feel his pulse starting to speed up as he walked towards the door.

Everything was OK. The only difference was that the room looked a lot cleaner than usual, and with a sigh Leo flopped down on his bed. He had some school work to do; better get on with it. And it was Art again tomorrow. He mustn't forget to take in the project stuff, or Ms Porter really *would* go off bang.

Grinning at the mental picture of Ms Porter exploding, Leo rummaged out his art, propped it up so he wouldn't forget it in the morning, then settled down to tonight's workload.

He'd been concentrating on history for about ten minutes when it happened.

Scritch. Scritch-scritch.

Leo raised his head very slowly, and stared at the wall.

Scritch. Scrabble-scrabble-scrabble.

His mouth tightened into a narrow, furious line.

Scrabble-scrabble.

They were managing not to giggle this time, and suddenly Leo saw red. He'd had *enough*! The twins would have to learn that they couldn't pester him the whole time – and they were going to get their first lesson right *now*!

He jumped up, and they must have heard him, because the scritching and scrabbling suddenly grew louder and more energetic. Seething, Leo headed for the door. As he passed his window, he heard high-pitched voices shouting and laughing outside, and glancing out he saw Thomas and Tina in the garden with Mum. They were all—

Hang on a minute!

Leo stopped in his tracks. The twins couldn't be in the garden with Mum. They were in their room, making stupid noises. He could *hear* them.

Thinking for a moment that he was going out of his mind, Leo looked towards the window again.

Thomas and Tina were outside.

So what was making that scratching noise?

6

Leo didn't think he was really chicken, but it took all the nerve he had to tiptoe the few steps along the landing to the next bedroom. He put his ear to the door, but he couldn't hear a sound. OK. Then there was only one thing for it.

He opened the door and marched in.

Beds. Shelves. Big cushions. Toys all over the floor. There was nothing else in there. Nothing moving; nothing going *scritch-scritch*. The twins didn't even have a ticking clock, because they couldn't tell the time yet.

So what *was* it?

Leo stared around the room. He still felt

nervous, even though there was nothing weird to see. And he knew he'd stay nervous until he got to the bottom of this mystery.

He started picking up the toys and looking at them, wondering if maybe some battery-driven thing had been left on. The noise had stopped now, so he had no way of knowing which direction it had been coming from. He *had* heard it, hadn't he? He hadn't imagined the whole thing, like Mikey had said about the spider on the screen?

Then just as he thought the words *spider on the screen*, he saw it.

It moved so fast that it was a blur at the corner of Leo's vision, but it made him jump as if something had bitten him. Over the carpet, round a stuffed doll that looked like it had had an argument with a ten-tonne truck, and like lightning into a shadowy corner.

Leo didn't see it clearly enough to be sure that it *was* a spider, but he'd have bet just about anything on it. He'd have bet a million pounds.

He ran to where it had vanished, got down on his knees and peered into the corner. It wasn't there; of course it wasn't. Like the one that had scared Mum last night, it had more sense than to hang around. But Leo *did* find one thing: a tiny gap in the skirting-board, just about big enough for it to have wriggled through.

Then, right on cue, he heard the noise again.

Scritch. Scritch. Scrabble-scrabble-scrabble.

It was coming from inside the wall, a few centimetres from his nose.

Leo stood up. Well, he'd solved the mystery, hadn't he? A jumbo-sized spider running around the house, scrabbling in the wall and then coming out when no one was around to make webs everywhere. Oh, great! Mum was going to *love* this!

Well, maybe the sensible thing was to do something about it before she found out. There was a can of insect spray downstairs – a squirt or two through the gap in the skirting-board should do the trick. It was probably the same spider that had been downstairs yesterday, so with any luck he'd solve two problems in one go. Yeah, that was the answer. *Go on, Leo*, he told himself. *Go and sort it out. You're not really feeling nervy, are you? Your heart isn't thudding for no reason. Go on. Get the spray. Do it now!*

Though he didn't know why, Leo's lips felt very dry. He licked them, but it didn't make a lot of difference. Prat! Of course he hadn't got the wind up. Why should he? It was only a spider after all.

All the same, he ran out of the twins' room and pounded down the stairs two at a time.

Five minutes later, he was on his way upstairs again. That bout of nerves had been completely stupid, but after sitting at the table for a bit and eating a couple of biscuits, he was feeling calmer. He'd found the insect spray, and was holding it in his hand like a weapon as he headed for Thomas and Tina's bedroom.

There was no sign of the spider. No scuttling shapes, no webs, no noises inside the wall. That made Leo feel even better, and he lay down flat on the carpet, wriggling until he could position the nozzle of the spray can right in front of the tiny hole.

"OK, punk!" he snarled, doing his best sci-fi cop impersonation. "Gedda loada *this*!"

S-ss-sss! The spray hissed into the hole, and Leo dodged back quickly before any could go up his nose. That was telling it! No more scritch-scrabbling. No more cobwebs. No more—

"What you doing?"

"Aaah!" Leo jumped as if someone had kicked him, and shot upright.

Thomas and Tina were standing behind him.

Thomas had his hands behind his back, Tina had one thumb in her mouth. They were both looking at him very suspiciously.

"Our room," said Thomas. "You're not 'lowed!"

"Of course I'm allowed!" Then the twins spotted the spray-can in his hand, and Tina pointed at it.

"What that?"

"It's . . . um . . . just something of mine."

Thomas shook his head. "Isn't!" he argued. "Mummy's. I *seen* it. It goes *ssss . . . ssss* an' then the flies all-fall-down-dead!" He paused. "Why *you* got it?"

Tina tried to grab the can, but Leo held it out of her reach. "No!" she shouted. "*Bad* Leebo! I'll tell Mummy!"

That was the last thing Leo wanted, so he thought he'd better level with the twins and try and make them understand. "Look," he said with a sigh, "I'm not doing anything bad! I'm just getting rid of a big, nasty old creepy-crawly. You don't want creepy-crawlies in your room, do you?"

They stared at him for a moment. Then Tina's face crumpled and she burst into noisy tears. "*Leebo hurt Incy!*" she howled. "*Bad Leebo, horrid, bad, BAD!*"

She flew at him like a small whirlwind, bashing at his legs with clenched fists, and Thomas joined in too, yelling, "*Bad, BAD!*" Leo was completely flummoxed. And so was Mum, who heard the noise from the garden and came rushing up the stairs.

"What on earth is going *on*?" she shouted above the din Thomas and Tina were making. "Leo, what have you done to them?"

"Nothing!" Leo protested. But he wasn't allowed to explain until Mum had calmed the twins down. She knew how to do it, too. A couple of pieces of chocolate, and they both stopped howling, as instantly as if someone had switched them off.

Leo blinked in the sudden silence. Thomas and Tina glowered at him. "Well?" said Mum menacingly.

She understood when he finally managed to explain. In fact she was glad he'd done it. It was just a shame that the twins had come in when they had, and that he'd been daft enough to tell them the truth.

"You can't tell them about killing pests," Mum said. "They're too young to understand. You should have made up some story."

Fat chance, in three seconds flat! Leo thought. But he didn't bother arguing. The spider was gone, and the twins'd soon forget all about it. And at least he was in Mum's good books for getting rid of it. It made a change to have done something right.

"Oh, well, I suppose I should think about getting tea ready," Mum said reluctantly. "And if you've got any homework, Leo, you'd better get on with it."

She left the room. The twins, who had heard the word "tea", started to follow her, then stopped at the door and stared back at Leo.

"Don't like you any more," said Tina.

"No, don't *like* you," agreed Thomas. Then, unexpectedly, he grinned. It wasn't a nice grin at all. In fact, it was downright *sinister*.

"Can't hurt Incy," he added, sounding smug. "*We* know."

"Yeah," Tina chimed in. "IncyWincyPider's our *friend*."

They both ran out and away along the landing. Leo felt a nasty little shiver run up his spine. What had they meant by *that*. . .?

"Oh, rats!" he suddenly said aloud. They were only kids. They talked garbage half the time anyway. And they were cross with him, so it was no wonder they were trying to give him the crawls. It didn't *mean* anything.

He turned and looked at the spot under the

skirting-board. There was a dark stain where he'd squirted the spray-can, and Leo smiled to himself.

"Down came the rain, and washed the spider out," he said with satisfaction. "Nah – I've sorted you out, haven't I? Bye bye, Incy Wincy. Bye bye for *good*!"

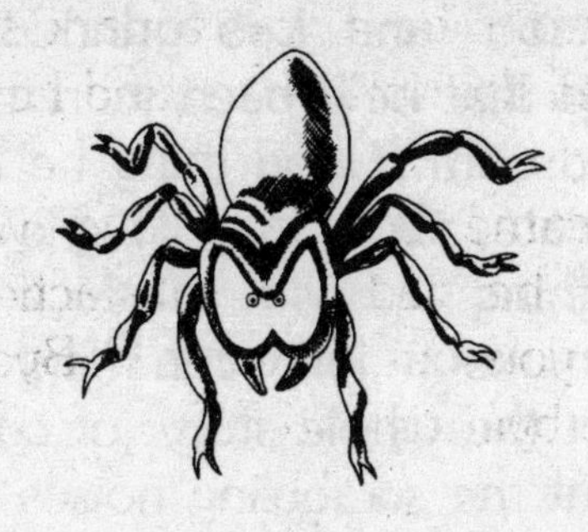

7

Next morning, Leo felt a lot better. His room wasn't filled with cobwebs when he woke up, there'd been no more scrabblings in the wall, and no trouble with the computer. The problem, it seemed, was solved.

On the way to school, he thought sensibly about it all. Obviously, there wasn't any connection between the bugged computer game and the real spider. It was just a coincidence that the two things had happened at the same time. He'd simply let himself get wound up about it. And the twins' passion for "Incy Wincy Spider" had blown the whole thing up in his mind.

Well, it was gone now. The creepy feelings

had gone, too, and Leo grinned when he remembered that he'd been scared to go into his own bedroom. Good thing he hadn't told any of his mates about that! They'd have rolled around laughing.

He did make a joky comment to Mikey, though. Not the whole story, of course – just the bit about the scrabbling noises and squirting the spray into the skirting-board. And what Mum had said about the number of spiders in the garden. But Mikey didn't seem interested and changed the subject.

When the time came for Art, Ms Porter was pleased to see that Leo had remembered to bring his project.

"Ah, good," she said, smiling at him. "Now, open your folder and let's see how you're getting on."

Leo opened the folder – and they both stared.

"What on *earth*. . .?" said Ms Porter.

Everything inside the folder was covered with cobwebs. Leo's pictures, his notes, his spare materials – they were all completely plastered with silvery-grey strands. The webs clung to Leo's fingers as he tried to pull them away. His classmates started to giggle. Then they started to laugh uproariously.

"It's not funny!" Ms Porter snapped. She turned on Leo. "What have you been *doing* to your work?"

"I haven't done anything!" Leo said in dismay. "Honest, Ms Porter, I don't know where this stuff came from!"

But he did know. Whatever it was that had caused havoc in his room had left its mark on the folder, too.

"Eeuch!" Ms Porter had a handful of the cobwebs now, and she pulled a face. "You'd better take it all outside and clean it up! Though how you could have let it get into such a state is beyond me!"

"Leo's got a little brother and sister, Ms Porter," said Mikey. "He told me they're always messing around with his things, so maybe it was them."

Leo looked at him in surprise. He'd certainly never said anything of the sort to Mikey, so why was Mikey suddenly pitching in on his side?

But whatever Mikey's reasons were, Ms Porter seemed to think it was a likely explanation. Leo mouthed "Thanks!" as he went out to get rid of the cobwebs, but Mikey didn't smile. In fact he was frowning, and Leo couldn't work out why.

He tried to talk to Mikey later, but it didn't work out. Mikey was always too busy, or with other people, and there was no chance to see him in private. It was almost as if he was avoiding Leo.

Oh, well. It was Friday, so he wouldn't see Mikey again until after the weekend. Forget about it, Leo told himself. Mikey was probably just in a weird mood.

Mum and Dad were going out again that evening, so for Leo it was babysitting time. To his surprise, the twins didn't play up at bedtime. Usually there was chaos and a lot of arguing, but tonight was different. They still didn't like their brother, and wouldn't talk to him much, but they behaved themselves and went to bed as good as gold.

Leo had a nasty feeling that they must be plotting something, but he decided not to worry. If they were going to make trouble, he'd deal with it when it happened. Until then, he'd enjoy the peace.

There was blissful silence from the next room when he settled down at his computer. The first thing he saw when he logged on to the Internet was an e-mail from Scott.

Hi, Leo, the message said. *Haven't heard*

from you in a while – hope things are OK there. I got some stuff from your friend Mikey. Oddball guy, or what? He sure has got a brain, though. Says he can write a program that KO's computer viruses, and know what, I believe him.

I mailed him back with some things I found out about that spider game. It's really bugging him, huh? (Hey, pun!) He must have some kinda thing about spiders. Anyways, he'll tell you what we said – saves me typing it twice. Stay cool, and mail back soon – Scott.

Leo was puzzled. What did Scott mean, *It's really bugging him*? And what sort of "thing" did he think Mikey had about spiders? Leo hadn't seen any sign of it. When he'd tried to tell him about what happened yesterday, Mikey hadn't even been interested. So what had he been saying to Scott?

He wondered whether to phone Mikey and ask him what was going on, but decided it wasn't worth the bother. He had much better things to do, so he settled down to see what was interesting on the Net.

He'd been flicking around some websites for ten minutes or so when he heard giggling from the twins' room. *Uh-oh!* He should have known this was too good to last. Leo paused, listening. From what he could tell, Thomas and Tina were playing a game that mostly involved pushing objects around and saying, "Wheeee!" Something was squeaking, too. It sounded like the wheels of their furry, push-along horse (which for some reason of their own they called Gondy). And every few moments one or the other of them would hiss: "*Shh!*"

Leo decided to leave them to it. It was a fairly quiet game, and they wouldn't come to any harm. Unless it sounded as if murder was being done, why not let them have their fun? At least they weren't chanting "Incy Wincy Spider"!

There wasn't anything really worth looking at on the Net, so after a few more minutes he went down to the kitchen for a snack and a drink. The squeaking and the "Wheee!" noises were still going on, but Thomas and Tina would get tired eventually. When they did, he could put them to bed, and then he'd clear up the mess they'd made.

He was having his second glass of orange juice (Mum had this health thing and rationed his cola) and looking at the TV page in the paper when there was an enormous *thump* from overhead.

"Oh, no!" Something had gone flying. Or someone had had an accident! Leo raced upstairs again. He expected to hear howling from the twins' bedroom. But it was quiet. *Too* quiet.

"Thomas! Tina!" He flung the door open. "What's up?"

Gondy the push-along horse was in the middle of the floor, lying on its side. The crash must have been it falling over. And there were his little brother and sister, squatting beside it. Tina was dangling something above Gondy's head – something that jiggled and joggled at the end of a string.

"Whatever are you two *doing*?" Leo demanded.

Tina ignored him, but Thomas looked up. "Go 'way!" he said firmly.

"No, I won't go away!" Leo retorted. "I want to know what you're up to!"

"Nuffing!"

That wasn't true, for starters. "Now, look!" Leo stamped across the room and reached for the horse's push handle, meaning to yank it upright again. As he grabbed it, Tina yelled, "*Leave-alone!*" and swiped at him with her free hand.

Then Leo saw what she was dangling over

the horse. It was a toy spider on a string – a big black spider, with felt eyes that looked like two fried eggs.

"*Where the heck did you get that?*" he yelped.

Tina scowled at him, and snatched the spider out of his reach. "Mine!" she said.

With an effort Leo got himself under control. "All right, all right, it's yours! But where did you *get* it?"

She didn't answer, but Thomas piped up proudly, "Playkool." He smirked at Leo. "IncyWincyPider!"

Oh, *wonderful*! They must have pinched it from the playschool toybox when no one was looking. "Now look," Leo said carefully, trying to sound all nice and reasonable. "If you took it from playschool, then it isn't really yours, is it?"

"Is!" said Tina.

"No, it isn't. So you'll have to put it back next time you go." Leo paused, then trundled out his big weapon. "Or I'll tell Mum."

Tina's mouth turned down at the corners. "Want to keep him," she said sulkily. "IncyWincyPider." She waggled the toy over the horse again and added, "IncyWincy got Gondy. Going to *eat* him!"

Leo made a grab for the spider and snatched it out of her hand. "Incy Wincy isn't going to eat anyone!" he growled, wishing that the jittery feeling he'd suddenly got would go away. "I've had enough! You two are going back to bed, and you're going right now!"

He expected Tina to kick up a fuss about having the spider taken away. To his surprise, though, she didn't. She muttered, "Don't like you any more!" again as Leo tucked her in bed, but that was all.

Until Leo turned to go out of the room. Then a small voice whispered: "*Don't care, anyway.*"

"What?" Leo paused.

Tina was looking at him from under the bed-covers. "Don't care," she repeated slyly. "Thomas and me got 'nother IncyWincy."

"Yeah," agreed Thomas. "*Proper* one." His small face broke into the same horrible, leering grin that he'd used yesterday. "He *still* lives in the wall. An' he's going to *get* you!"

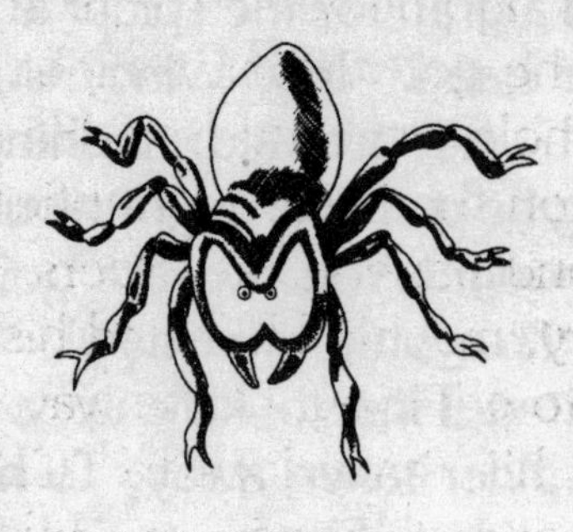

8

Leo put the toy spider in a carrier bag and stuffed it away at the bottom of his cupboard. He didn't want to look at it. He'd had enough of spiders to last him a year!

All the same, he couldn't stop himself from wondering if, maybe, the real spider *was* still around. He could have missed with the spray can. Or it could be SuperInsect – one of those ones that pesticides didn't knock over any more. Leo didn't like that thought, and hurriedly pushed it away. Nah. He hadn't heard a sound from inside the wall since yesterday. The twins had just been winding him up. No possible doubt about it – that thing was gone.

OK, then. Homework. He didn't relish the idea, but if he got it done tonight, that would leave the whole weekend free. He dumped his school bag on the bed and emptied it, scattering books and papers and folders. What to do first? History, maybe. He hated history, so it'd be brilliant to get it out of the way.

He put his encyclopedia CD into the computer and started to hunt through the index for the information he wanted. He was absorbed (or sort of) in the search when he heard something.

A small scuffling noise.

In the wall.

Leo whirled round so fast on his swivel chair that he nearly turned a complete circle.

Scritch-scritch. Scrabble. . .

He was on his feet in an instant and hurrying to the spot where the sound was coming from. Getting down on his knees, he pressed his ear to the wall near floor level. If it was the twins, he'd surely hear them muttering and whispering.

He didn't. All he heard was that furtive noise: *scritch-scritch, scrabble-scrabble.*

Something was very definitely moving around in there.

And, though he didn't like to admit it one bit,

Leo couldn't get rid of the feeling that it sounded *bigger* than before.

His heart was bumping as he went next door to the twins' bedroom. There was still a chance that it *was* them, and if he crept in quietly he'd catch them at it. In which case he'd have their guts on a plate. But a small voice inside him was saying, *Not a chance, Leo*. And the voice was right. When he peeked into the room, he saw the twins sound asleep in bed.

While behind the skirting-board, something scuffled and scrabbled and scuttered.

He eased out of the room – then suddenly common sense took a hand. This was *stupid*. What on earth was he doing, getting the jitters? All it meant was that he hadn't got rid of the spider and it was still hanging around. Or maybe it wasn't even the spider at all; maybe there was a mouse in the house. It certainly sounded loud enough to be a mouse, didn't it? Yeah. That was the answer. They'd got a mouse.

Well, Dad could deal with that. Set a trap, or get a cat (a cat would be nice to have around anyway). Problem solved. Easy. Yeah.

Telling himself that he felt better, he went back to his own room.

He'd taken one step over the threshold when he heard music.

Uh? Leo thought. It was only a few notes, but it had come from his computer speakers – and it was familiar. For a moment he couldn't remember where he'd heard it before. Then it clicked. And he ran to look at his screen.

The encyclopedia index had vanished. In its place, bouncing and jiggling in the middle of the picture, was the cartoon spider.

"*No!*" Leo yelled, aghast. "You can't have come back!"

The spider jiggled more madly than ever as a burst of cackling, tinny laughter erupted from the speakers. Then, as Leo stood frozen with shock, the spider started to dart all over the screen. As it went, black threads came spinning out behind it – and the threads were forming words. There were just five of them. They said:

I'LL GET YOU FOR THAT.

The spider gave one last cackle, and shot away offscreen. For a few seconds the message stayed, the letters joggling as if something was shaking them. Then they faded . . . faded . . . and disappeared.

Leo sat down on his bed with a thump that shook the floor. The computer screen looked perfectly normal now. The encyclopedia was back, and there was no sign of the spider or its web. Frantically, he tried to grab hold of the thought that he'd imagined it all, and the ominous message hadn't really been there. But he couldn't make himself believe that. He'd seen the message with his own eyes. It *was* real!

He didn't want to touch the computer, but he made himself do it, shutting it down and switching it off as quickly as he could. Then he got on the phone.

Mikey was in, but as soon as he heard Leo's voice, he started to sound wary. He didn't really want to listen to Leo's story, but Leo didn't give him a chance to get away. He told him everything – the noises in the wall, the cobwebs, and, finally, the menacing threat that had appeared on his screen.

"I'm not saying you didn't get rid of that virus," he finished, trying to keep his voice steady. "I know you did. I *believe* you. But . . . it's come back. Or –" He swallowed, not sure if he could say what he really wanted to. But he had to. "Or – *something* has," he finished.

There was a long silence. At last, wondering if they'd been cut off, Leo said, "Mikey?"

"Yeah, I'm here. Look, Leo, this is *crazy*.

There can't be anything left inside your computer. There just can't, OK?"

"I *know*," said Leo desperately, "but—"

"So now you're telling me that there's some spooky spider running round your house, and then the computer spider showed up again, and it wrote this spooky message on the screen. Well, *I'm* telling *you* it can't have done, 'cause it isn't *there*." He paused. "You're winding me up, aren't you? This is some sort of dumb game to make me look a prat—"

"It isn't! Honest, Mikey, cross my heart! There *is* something weird going on, and – and I'm *scared*!" Leo took a deep breath. "Mikey, can you – I mean, couldn't you come over here?"

"No," Mikey retorted instantly. "I'm busy, and it's too late. Mum and Dad wouldn't let me. Anyway, what's there to see?"

Leo didn't have an answer to that. There was another pause. Then Mikey said, in a slightly different tone, "Look, why not e-mail your friend Scott? Tell him about it. He might have some ideas."

"Scott?" Leo echoed, baffled. "What does he know about this?"

"I didn't say he knows anything about it. I just said why don't you e-mail him. I've got to go now. Dad wants to use the phone."

"*Mikey—*"

"Bye," said Mikey, and hung up.

Leo didn't understand. Why didn't Mikey want to talk about the problem? Only a day or two ago he'd been really enthusiastic, and now suddenly he'd changed. What was going on in Mikey's head?

He remembered Scott's remark that Mikey must have "some kinda thing" about spiders. What did that mean? Maybe he *should* e-mail Scott, and see what he could find out.

If only he wasn't too scared to use the computer. . .

He was still dithering about whether to switch on again when there was a patter of feet and the twins appeared in the doorway.

"We woked up," said Tina.

"Yeah," said Thomas. "Why was you shouting?"

"I wasn't shouting, I was talking to someone on the phone," Leo told them. "Go back to bed."

"Don't want to. We got somefing. Leebo come 'n' see."

They seemed to have forgotten that they didn't like him any more. Leo sighed. "I don't want to come and see anything, and you're supposed to be asleep. Go on, or Mum'll be cross."

"Won't," Tina retorted. "You come 'n' see what we got." She waggled her fingers. "IncyWincy gived it us."

Leo's stomach lurched. What did she mean?

"Yeah," Thomas agreed, nodding. "Like this. Look!"

He held up both hands. They were covered with cobwebs.

He shot past the twins so fast that he nearly knocked them flying. Their bedroom door was wide open. The nightlight shone, and for a moment he thought everything was all right.

Then he saw Gondy, the toy horse.

Thomas's voice behind him said proudly, "Incy maked it!" but Leo could only stare.

Gondy stood in the middle of the room. At least, he thought it must be Gondy. But it wasn't easy to be sure.

Because Gondy was totally wrapped in a thick layer of cobwebs.

9

Mum and Dad got home just as Leo was lugging the toy horse through the kitchen. Hastily, he shoved Gondy under the table, then went into the hall in time to hear the key turn in the lock. While he was saying "Hi", and trying to act as if nothing had happened, the twins came thundering downstairs.

"Mummy, Mummy!" Tina shrieked happily. "We been playing IncyWincyPider!"

"*Real* IncyWincy!" Thomas added, "An' he maked us a 'pider's web!"

"Leo, what are they doing out of bed?" Mum shouted above the racket.

Leo spread his hands helplessly. "They just

woke up, and I couldn't get them back to sleep."

"IncyWincy, IncyWincy!" chanted Tina. "Up'tairs in our room! Come 'n' see!"

Mum groaned. "All right, I'll sort them out. Put the kettle on, Leo."

Luckily, the twins were so excited that she thought they were talking gibberish. She chivvied them up the stairs – then, as all three disappeared, Dad called out from the kitchen.

"Leo! What on earth's *this* doing here?"

He'd spotted Gondy.

Leo explained that he'd found the horse covered in cobwebs, adding – honestly – that he didn't have the foggiest idea how it had happened. When he'd finished, Dad frowned at Gondy. "That *is* strange," he said. "I didn't think spiders could work so fast."

"Right," Leo agreed. He shuffled from one foot to the other. "And – um – there's something else."

"Oh?" Dad looked suspicious.

"Yeah. That one that scared Mum the other day – I don't think I got it with the spray. I think it's still around."

"Oh," Dad said again. Leo wished he'd say something useful instead. He desperately wanted to tell Dad the real story – all of it – and ask him for help. But what was the point? He might as well try to make Dad believe that the world was flat and the next-door neighbours were Martians.

"Well," Dad said, "we'd better get all this stuff cleaned off before Mum comes down and sees it. And don't say anything about the spider, all right? She'll only start getting jumpy."

She's not the only one, Leo thought, but he didn't say it aloud. They cleaned the worst of the cobwebs from Gondy, then Dad took the toy horse outside and walloped him a few times to get rid of the rest. He came back in looking cheerful and said the twins could have their toy back in the morning and he just hoped the spider wouldn't go and do it again. He didn't sound the least bit worried, just curious. And that didn't help Leo at all.

Leo was very unwilling to go to bed that night. He found all kinds of reasons to stay up, until it was so late that even Dad (who didn't usually notice) told him to go upstairs and get some sleep.

"In a minute," Leo said.

Mum looked up. "Not 'in a minute', Leo – *now*. You heard what Dad said."

Leo didn't want to go. But he'd run out of

excuses. "Ohh . . . all right," he said reluctantly. He shuffled to the sitting-room door and hung around with his hand on the handle. "Night, then."

"Night, Leo," said Dad.

"Go *on*," said Mum.

Leo opened the door but didn't go through it. "There's this programme on in ten minutes—" he began.

"No," said Mum.

It was useless. His bedroom – and whatever might or might not be lurking there – was waiting for him, and there was no hope of escape. Leo swallowed, hard. Then he took a deep breath, and made himself walk towards the stairs.

There wasn't anything horrible waiting for him in his room. No sign of any cobwebs. His computer hadn't switched itself on again. And there were no scritch-scrabbling noises in the walls. Leo got into bed, and in spite of his fears he was sound asleep in a few minutes.

But though there was nothing real to scare him, his dreams were another matter.

In the first one, he was trying desperately to climb up the drainpipe outside the house. It was dark, and though he couldn't see properly, he knew that *something* was crawling up the wall after him. Something with a lot of teeth, that cackled madly. If he could only reach his bedroom window, Leo knew he'd be safe. But he couldn't get a proper grip on the pipe. He kept sliding backwards. And the thing below him was creeping closer, *closer*, CLOSER—

He jolted awake, and lay curled up with his head under the duvet until he was convinced that the dream really had gone. Even when he *was* convinced, he got out of bed and padded to the window, peering down to where the drainpipe showed faintly in the glow of the street lamps. Just to make sure.

Leo returned to bed and managed to get back to sleep. And then he had the second dream.

It involved the drainpipe again. But this time, he wasn't trying to climb up the outside. Instead, he'd shrunk to about ten centimetres tall, and he was *inside* the pipe, scrambling and slithering through dank, slippery darkness. He had to reach the top. He wasn't allowed to stop till he did. But there were no foot- or hand-holds – though he kicked and scrabbled frantically, he was getting nowhere. And all the time, dinning in his ears, there was a sound like a huge echo of someone slowly chanting:

"*Incy Wincy SPIDER, climbing up the SPOUT!*
Incy Wincy SPIDER, climbing up the SPOUT!"

On and on it went, until Leo thought he'd go mad. "Stop it!" he yelled in his dream. "I'm doing my best! Stop that noise, just *stop*!"

"*Incy Wincy SPIDER, climbing up the SPOUT!*" chanted the voice relentlessly. Then, suddenly, the words changed.

"*Down came the RAIN*. . ." There was a cackle. And ahead of him, further up the pipe, Leo heard an ominous gurgling sound. . .

"*And washed the spider . . . OUT!*"

The last word turned into a hoot of laughter. Then the laughter was eclipsed by an enormous *WHOOSH* – and a wall of water came hurtling down the pipe, rushing at Leo like a tidal wave. Leo's eyes bulged, his mouth opened – he screamed in terror.

As the water hit him, he woke again.

"*Urrrh!*" He sat up, pushing both hands through his hair and then rubbing his eyes hard. That was a *stinker* of a dream! Well, he wasn't going to risk another one like that. He'd stay awake – read or something until it got light. He wasn't really tired anyway, not now.

Feeling a bit shaky, he switched his bedside

lamp on and settled down with a book. After five minutes, he started yawning. After ten minutes, his eyelids began to droop. After fifteen minutes, he was fast asleep once more.

And then he had the third dream, which was the worst one of all.

Leo dreamed that he was caught in a spider's web. He didn't know how he'd got there, but he was stuck fast, dangling in the strands with his arms and legs spreadeagled. At first he thought he could escape, but when he tried, he found that any kind of movement only made things worse. The web clung to him like a sticky tangle of Sellotape, and the more he wriggled and writhed, the more enmeshed he became. Before long he was wrapped up like a cocoon – he couldn't even move his legs now, and one arm was pinned to his side. He had to get out of this!

"Help!" he shouted. "Somebody, help!"

No one answered him, and when he looked around, all he could see was the web, stretching away in every direction.

He tried again. "Help! Anyone. . .?"

Nothing.

Except . . . the web was *moving* now. Jiggling and vibrating. It had done that when he'd tried to escape, but he wasn't trying to escape any more.

So what was making it shake?

An awful foreboding feeling made Leo turn his head . . . and he saw something coming towards him. It advanced very slowly, and he couldn't make out what it was. But it was big and bulgy, and there seemed to be several long, thin stalks coming out from it.

Stalks? Or legs?

"Oh, no-o-o!" Leo whispered. He could hear a sound now, muffled and faint, but getting louder. To begin with it seemed to be just a noise, like a long, drawn-out *Oooooo . . . Oooooo . . .* repeated over and over again. But then it became clearer. It was a word. A single word.

"*SOOOON . . . SOOOON. . .*"

Screaming was about the only thing Leo could do, and he did it. In fact he actually woke up shouting, though the sound he made was muffled by the duvet, which had somehow got itself over his head again. He kicked and wriggled, trying to throw the cover off.

But instead, he burst *through* it, and was sitting up in bed before he realized what was happening.

And when he did realize, he nearly screamed again.

What had covered him wasn't the duvet. It was cobwebs.

"*Uggh!*" Leo flung himself out of bed, dancing around and flailing his arms as he tried to tear the horrible sticky strands away. The web was on his skin, on his clothes, in his hair – and it was all over his bed, too, coating it like a thick blanket. In his panic to get it off, he tripped over his own feet and fell to the floor. He rolled over – and as he did so, he found himself looking upwards.

His heart nearly stopped beating. There were more cobwebs on the ceiling, and, in very large letters, they spelled out a word.

The word gave Leo a clear and menacing message. It was:

SOON.

10

It took half an hour under the shower before Leo was absolutely convinced that the last traces of cobwebs were gone. Even then, when he finally came out he kept thinking he could still *feel* them tickling his skin. He couldn't stop shaking. He was scared.

And he didn't know what to do.

He'd cleaned the mess in his room, dumping all the yukky stuff out of the window before he'd escaped to the bathroom. Now, coming out in jeans and T-shirt, he hung around on the landing. It was still only six o'clock in the morning, but no way was he going back to bed after what had happened. The way he was feeling right now, he'd probably never want to go to bed ever again.

The worst thing had been that word on the ceiling. SOON. It was a howlingly obvious threat. And the fact that he'd heard the same word in his nightmare gave it an extra, horrible emphasis. Whatever he was up against, it wasn't an ordinary spider. It was something much, *much* weirder and nastier.

He wondered if he dared sneak a look in the twins' room, and if he did, what he'd find. That business with Gondy the toy horse. . . If Thomas and Tina had been older, he might have suspected that they were faking the whole thing to scare the daylights out of him. Some joke-shop cobweb spray, a few scratching and scrabbling noises, and hey presto – one terrified big brother! But that wasn't possible. Thomas and Tina just couldn't have done it.

All the same, Leo was certain that the twins were involved in some way. They'd chattered on last night about "playing" with Incy Wincy Spider, and being "given" all the spider's webs. So they must have *seen* something – and unlike him, they thought it was loads of fun. If only he could talk to them properly. But that was no good, because they weren't old enough to understand the questions he wanted to ask, let alone give him an answer that made any sense.

Did he want to look in their room? Leo decided he didn't. All right, he was being chicken. But if anything else had happened in there, he didn't want to be the one who found out about it. He'd go and sit downstairs, he decided, and watch Breakfast TV till Mum and Dad got up. It would be boring, but it had to be better than going back to his room. *Anything* was better than that.

He mooched down the stairs. His bedroom door was shut, and everything in there was clean and tidy now. It was all very quiet.

At first.

Then something moved in a corner. It paused for a moment, then scurried quickly along the bottom of the wall that divided Leo's room from the twins'. It reached one leg of Leo's desk and paused again. Then it ran up the leg and over the top of the desk until it came to Leo's computer. It paused a third time, as if it was thinking about something. And then it scuttled round the back of the computer.

A minute later, the computer made a single bleeping noise. It shouldn't have been able to do that, because it wasn't switched on. Nothing else happened.

But the small, scuttling thing that had disappeared round the back of the machine didn't emerge on the other side.

". . . So now it's over to Terry for our wildlife spot," said the TV announcer cheerily. "And this morning we've got a special guest in the studio. Her name's Rosie, and she's got a lot more than two legs, and though she isn't very big, she certainly scares me! Because Rosie is – " pause for breath, big grin – "a tarantula spider!"

"Aagh, no!" Leo leaped for the remote control and switched the TV off. That was just about the last straw! Shivering, he went to the kitchen to get himself a third bowl of cereal. Eating seemed to help. It made him feel *normal*.

He was scraping the last bits from his bowl when he heard feet on the stairs, and moments later Mum came in.

"Good grief!" she said. "Whatever's got *you* up so early?"

Leo shrugged. "I woke up and didn't feel like sleeping any more."

"Oh, well. Makes a change. I hope you haven't eaten all the cornflakes." She poured herself a bowlful, went to the sink to fill the kettle, then suddenly jerked back. "Oh, *no*!"

"What's up?" Leo asked.

Mum pointed. "There's a spider!" she said in a squeamish voice. "Right there on the tap. Look – it's making itself a web! Oh, get rid of it, Leo, quickly!"

It was only a little one, but as he caught it in a tumbler and put it outside, Leo's heart thumped crazily. He couldn't get away from them! It was as if some evil force was sending armies of spiders to follow him around and taunt him at every opportunity!

He cringed as he watched the latest spider scurry away into the garden. At this rate he was going to end up with a phobia like Mum's! The only difference was, he had a good reason. . .

"Has it gone?" Mum asked as he went back to the kitchen.

Leo nodded. "Yeah."

"Good! Do you want some tea?"

She knew Leo didn't like tea, but she always asked. "No thanks," he said. Then he added, trying to sound casual, "Are the twins awake yet?"

"I don't know, I haven't looked," said Mum. "I expect—"

She was interrupted by a shout from

upstairs. "Mu-ummy! *Muuuu-ummy!*"

"Oh." Mum's face fell. "Well, there's your answer. Blast! I thought I might have a few more minutes' peace."

"*Muuu-uuummy!*"

Mum sighed and headed for the stairs. As she went up, Leo heard the twins' voices. They weren't shouting for her now. They were singing. He knew the song. He knew it very well.

"Incy Wincy Pider, climbing up the POUT!"

Leo covered his ears with his hands and pretended he wasn't listening.

He had to go back to his room, of course. It was his room, after all, and he couldn't move out of it and go somewhere else. There wasn't anywhere else to go. None the less, it took all the nerve he had to face it again. And when he did, he wasn't satisfied until he'd checked every corner and drawer and cupboard, and was sure that nothing lurked in any of them.

At last he started to feel better about being in there. Until, that was, he remembered his homework. The history project. The encyclopedia CD.

And what had happened when he'd tried to use it yesterday evening.

He could see the cartoon spider and its message again in his mind's eye, as clearly as if they were still glaring from the screen at him. I'LL GET YOU FOR THAT. And this morning, written on the ceiling in cobwebs, the word SOON. The link between them was all too obvious. I'LL GET YOU. . . What was it going to do? What was it *capable* of doing?

And what would he find waiting for him when he switched his computer on again?

Leo knew he couldn't put the awful moment off for ever. So wasn't it better to do it now, before his nerve failed? Otherwise, he'd tie himself in knots wondering.

He gritted his teeth, and pressed the ON button.

The computer made its usual noises as it started up. And to Leo's surprise and huge relief, everything was OK. He looked at his watch. Half-past ten. If he got on with that history stuff now, then maybe this afternoon he could go to the recreation ground. Some of his mates were sure to be up there, and he could have a bit of fun and just *forget* about spiders for a while.

He had another attack of nerves as he started up the encyclopedia. But nothing strange happened, and soon he was at work on his project. He could hear the twins playing in the garden. Good. That meant they wouldn't come pestering him. Now, if he could just find that entry he was looking for. . .

Bleep! Biddle-iddle-URP!

Leo jumped as the speakers came to life with an extraordinary noise. He stared at the screen. Nothing odd there, so what on earth—

Bing-bong! the computer announced. Then: "*Hello, Leo!*"

"What the—"

"*Hel-LO, Leo!*"

Two eyes were blinking at him from the bottom left-hand corner of the screen. They looked like a pair of fried eggs. And a long black leg was waving a greeting.

Leo made a gargling sound, jumped from his chair and backed away across the room. The cartoon spider scurried into full view. It did a little dance in the middle of the screen, then a burst of the tinny music he'd heard before blared from the speakers. When he'd first heard that music, Leo had thought it was stupid and pathetic. He didn't think it any more.

"*I'm going to get you!*" chortled the spider. "*Soon, soon, soon-soon-SOON!*"

"No!" Leo protested. "You can't! You're not real! Go away!"

"*Soon-soon-SOON! Soon-soon-VERY-soon!*" The spider jiggled madly, then turned a somersault and hung upside down on the screen, grinning madly at him. "*Incy Wincy Spider, climbing up the spout!*" it chanted.

Leo let out a yell. He didn't even bother to switch the computer off; he just grabbed the electric plug and yanked it out of its socket. The music died, the screen went blank, and the machine shut down. But Leo wasn't there to see it. He was already pounding along the landing towards the stairs.

"Leo?" Mum called as he rushed past her like a whirlwind. "Where are you going?"

"Er – just out!" Leo shouted back, sprinting through the back door. "Bike ride!"

"Well, don't be late for lunch!"

He didn't answer, and Mum shook her head despairingly. From the garden, Thomas and Tina saw Leo grab his bike and go hurtling out of the gate on it. They stared solemnly after him, then Thomas said, "Leebo's *scared*."

"Yeah," said Tina, nodding. "Scared of IncyWincy." She waggled her fingers and they both giggled.

They looked very *pleased* with themselves.

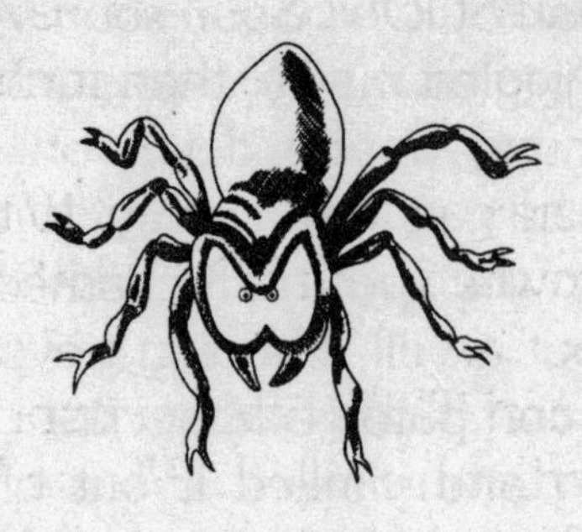

11

Leo had never been to Mikey's house before, but he knew Mikey's parents by sight, and Mrs Morris recognized him as she opened the door.

"Leo!" she said. "What a nice surprise. Have you come to see Mikey?"

Leo gulped, trying to get his breath back after the hectic bike ride. "Y-yes, Mrs Morris," he said. "Is he in?"

"He's in his room, playing with his computer as usual," she smiled. "Go on up. Second door on the right. He'll be pleased to see you."

I don't think he will, Leo thought, but only said thanks and ran up the stairs.

Mikey *wasn't* pleased to see him. It was

written all over his face as Leo barged into his room. But Leo didn't give him a chance to say anything.

"Mikey," he gasped, "I've got to talk to you!"

Mikey frowned warily. "What about? I'm busy—"

"I don't care! This is more important!" Leo's fists clenched at his sides. "*Please!*"

"Oh, hell!" said Mikey in a hollow voice. "All right. Shut the door. And then you'd better sit down before you fall down."

Leo shut the door, then flopped on to Mikey's bed. There was an amazing picture of the space shuttle on his computer screen, but Leo hardly noticed it.

"OK," said Mikey in a resigned sort of voice. "So tell. What's this all about?"

"Spiders," said Leo.

"Ah." Mikey clicked his mouse and the shuttle picture vanished. "I thought it might be."

Leo swallowed. "So you *do* know something!" Suddenly he felt angry. "Why wouldn't you talk to me about it before? What's the matter with you?"

Mikey didn't answer for a while. Then he said, "I'm scared, mate. That's what."

"Scared?" Leo echoed. "Of—"

"Spiders. If you want the real truth, I'm *terrified* of them. I can't even look at one without freaking out."

"You mean, you're like my mum? You've got ara – ara –"

"Arachnophobia. That's the word for it." Mikey shrugged. "Just one of those things."

"Why didn't you *tell* me?"

Mikey shrugged again. "Who wants to admit they're a wimp? You'd have laughed."

"I would *not*!" said Leo hotly. "Especially not now, after the things that've happened to me!"

"Well, I didn't know that, did I?" Mikey heaved a big sigh. "Look, I'm sorry. Truth is, when I started to realize what was going on, I got the wind up. First there was that Incy Wincy game. Then there was what happened in Art, with your project folder. Then that crazy stuff you told me on the phone, and after what I'd heard from Scott—"

"From *Scott*?"

Mikey looked sideways at him. "Haven't you had an e-mail from him lately?"

"I don't know. I haven't checked for a few days."

"Oh. Well, maybe you'd better."

Feeling that he was close to exploding, Leo said, "Mikey, just tell me what's going *on*!

What's Scott *said* to you?"

But Mikey shook his head. "I'll explain later," he said firmly. "First, I think you'd better tell me what *you* know. Start right at the beginning. That's usually the best place."

So Leo did. In fact, he told Mikey absolutely everything. Even if Mikey thought he was mad, just to be able to *say* what had happened, out loud and to another person, was an enormous relief.

Mikey was a good listener. He didn't interrupt once as the tale came out. And when Leo finished, all he said was, "*Whoooo!*"

Leo waited. He wondered what Mikey was thinking. At last he couldn't stand it any longer.

"You don't believe me, do you?" he burst out.

Mikey sat hunched up on his chair. "A couple of days ago I wouldn't have done. Now, though. . ." He reached to a pile of papers next to his computer and handed one to Leo. "You'd better read this."

It was a printout of an e-mail from Scott. And what Scott had to say sent a chill down Leo's spine.

Hi, Mikey. Got your last mail. Yeah, there's

some news this end, though it's pretty weird and I don't know what to make of it.

You know I told you some of the other guys in school downloaded this Incy program and had the same trouble Leo did. Well, one of those guys didn't show up in class one day, and next thing we heard his folks are selling up and moving away upstate. They took him out of school, their house is empty, and they're GONE. Story is that they suddenly got this mega-invasion of – you guessed it – spiders. And these spiders were BIG and they were doing things spiders shouldn't be able to do.

So yesterday me and a coupla guys went over to the empty house. The outside looked real scrubby and dusty, and then we took a look through the windows. Know what we saw in there? Yeah, you guessed right again – spider webs. And I mean EVERYWHERE. The place looks like it hasn't been lived in for about five thousand years. Is this serious weirdness, or is it not?

I don't know what happened in that house and I don't really want to know. But I haven't heard from Leo in a while. I've sent him messages but got no answer, and I'm getting kinda worried. Is he OK? Let me know soon as you can, huh? And get back to me about the program stuff we talked about. I'm starting to feel a bit nervous about this, know what I mean?

Hang in there – Scott.

Leo put the paper down. His hand was shaking. "Oh, God!" he said in a very small voice.

"Yeah," said Mikey. "Like Scott says, serious weirdness." He looked at Leo. "I got that message this morning, and when I read it I thought: Mikey, you're being a real scumbag, bottling out when Leo needs you. So when you turned up, I was sitting here trying to work up the nerve to phone you." He blinked and tried to smile, though it wasn't very successful. "Looks like you've saved me the trouble."

Leo was beginning to feel queasy with nerves himself. "So you'll help?" he asked.

Mikey nodded. "Yeah. At least, I'll try. Though if we had to face anything like Scott saw in his friend's house, I'd – well, I've told you. I couldn't handle it."

Leo understood. "Let's hope we won't have to," he said, "'cause I don't think I could handle it, either."

Neither of them wanted to go back to Leo's

house, but there was no choice. If they were going to face up to this, they couldn't do it from a distance. All the same, they cycled very slowly, and when they reached the front gate they hung around outside for some time, as if just looking at the house would help solve their problem. But it didn't help, and at last they went in.

They met Leo's dad in the hall. He had a vague expression on his face, which meant he'd been working. When he saw Mikey he said, "Oh – hello. Tim, isn't it?"

"Mikey," said Mikey.

"Mikey, yes. Of course. How are you? Good." Dad disappeared into his study.

Mikey smothered a grin, then asked, "You sure your parents won't mind me hanging around?"

"They probably won't even *notice*," Leo told him. "Come on. We'd better go up to my room and see if anything else has happened."

It hadn't, yet. But what they found when they opened the door was a pretty good recipe for disaster.

Thomas and Tina were in Leo's room. They were huddled together in front of his computer, and the computer was switched on.

"Hey!" Leo charged across the room,

grabbed the nearest twin – who was Tina – and hauled her away. "What do you think you're doing? You know you're not allowed to touch that!"

Tina kicked him. "Wasn't!" she yelled.

"Yes you was – I mean, were! I just came in and *caught* you!"

Cornered, Tina tried to change her story. "Wasn't *me*," she pouted. "Thomas doned it."

"Didn't!" protested Thomas, coming out from under the desk, where he'd been trying to hide. He looked at Leo, then suddenly beamed. "We was playing wiv Incy. He went in *there*."

And he pointed to the computer screen.

Leo's stomach felt as if he'd just swallowed an enormous lump of ice. "*What?*" he hissed.

Mikey, meanwhile, wasn't listening. He was clicking Leo's mouse and watching the screen intently. "I think it's OK," he said. "I don't think they've done any damage."

But Leo wasn't interested in what the twins had or hadn't done. He'd seen something on his desk. It looked like a fuzzy grey film, and it stretched across the desk top and behind the computer.

"Mikey. . ." he said shakily.

Mikey looked up. "No, really, it *is* OK," he

repeated. "Luckily, they didn't—" He stopped. "Oh-oh!"

"Right." Leo licked his lips, then cautiously reached out and prodded at the grey film. He knew the feel of it, all right. And it hadn't been there earlier this morning.

With his legs like jelly, he turned to face Thomas and Tina. "Now listen," he said, speaking very slowly and trying not to scream at them. "What did you mean when you said Incy went in there?"

Thomas nodded happily. "Did," he replied.

Leo's nerves were stretching tighter and tighter. "Yeah, I *know* he did. But *how*?"

Thomas shrugged. "Dunno. Just did."

Tina piped up. "He went *wheeee*!" she told Leo, skittering her fingers across the desk. "An' then he went—" Her hand hovered by the back of the computer – "*whum*!" Like lightning she swiped at the machine, missing the mains plug by a millimetre. "Incy's *clever*," she finished.

Incy certainly was. Because no way would a real spider have gone in there.

"I think," Mikey said uneasily, "that you ought to shut this computer down. Unplug it, too. And then I think I ought to take the cover off and see if there really *is* anything inside.

'Cause if there isn't—"

He was interrupted by a noise from the speakers.

Biddle-iddle-EEEP!

Mikey said "Aah!" and jerked backwards. And from the speakers came something that Leo had heard before.

Bing-bong!

"*Hel-LO, Leo! I'm back!*"

12

The spider was on the screen, cavorting from side to side. Leo took one look and yelled, "*Turn it off!*"

He leaped for the button, but Mikey snatched at his arm. "No!" he shouted. "Don't – not yet!"

He grabbed hold of both speaker leads and pulled the plugs out. The awful cackling that had started to blare through the room crashed into silence – and the spider on the screen stopped dancing. It stared out at them. It blinked. Then it showed its jagged cartoon teeth in a silent but unmistakable snarl.

"That's given it something to think

about. . ." Mikey's face had gone pale, but he was firmly telling himself that the spider was only an animated picture and not real.

Incy Wincy snarled again. Then he scurried to the left side of the screen. Four of his eight legs became a blur as he started to scribble spider-web words.

SOON. SOON. SOON.

Leo's teeth started to chatter. Incy paused, leered at him and scribbled again.

I'LL GET YOU, I'LL GET YOU! TIME'S RUNNING OUT! VERY SOON, VERY SOON, VERY VERY SOON!

Mikey hissed, "Move over!"

Leo was standing numbly in front of the screen, and only moved when Mikey shoved him. He wasn't aware of the twins gleefully bouncing and chuckling and clapping their hands. He just stared, like someone in a trance, as Mikey slid on to the swivel chair.

Mikey's fingers poised over the computer keyboard and he started to type. The letters he was typing should have appeared on the screen, but they didn't.

"Blast!" said Mikey. He tried again, but still nothing came up. "Something's blocking it out!"

The spider leaped up and down. Its teeth

gnashed and its whole body quivered, as if it was laughing madly. The twins laughed, too – and suddenly Leo snapped out of his trance. Rounding on them, he barked, "Shut up! Just *shut up*!"

Tina stuck her tongue out at him. "Don't care! You tried to hurt Incy!"

"Yeah!" yelled Thomas. "An' Incy'll *get* you!"

That did it. Leo gave a wordless yell and pounced on the computer. Before Mikey could protest, he'd hit the OFF button, so hard that he almost sent the machine skidding off the desk. The cartoon spider opened its mouth one last time –

Then the picture went blank.

Leo and Mikey both stared at the darkened screen, though there was nothing to see now. The twins stared, too. They looked disappointed. Thomas said accusingly, "Leebo spoiled it!"

Leo shut his eyes. "Get out!" he told them through clenched teeth. "Just get *out* of here!"

For a moment it seemed that they wouldn't. But then Tina stuck her tongue out at him again, and as one the twins bolted for the door. Leo slammed it shut behind them. He heard them giggling outside. Then they ran away along the landing.

"Oh, God!" He slumped on to his bed and hid his face in his hands. "I'm scared, Mikey. I'm really *scared*!"

Mikey was still looking at the computer, and frowning. "I don't get it," he said. "The things I was typing should have shown up on the screen."

"Well, they didn't!" Leo uncovered his face and looked up. "What were they anyway?"

"I was trying to talk to it."

"You were *what*?"

"Trying to talk to it," Mikey repeated. "Look, it keeps sending all these messages to you, doesn't it? So I thought, what if we try to talk back? If we could get some sort of communication going—"

"Hang on," Leo interrupted. "What exactly did you say to it?"

Mikey looked a bit embarrassed. "Well . . . I couldn't think of anything really useful off the top of my head. So I tried to put: 'Get lost'. Only nothing showed on the screen."

"'Get lost'!" said Leo. "Oh, *brilliant*! I mean, that really helps, doesn't it?"

"OK, so you do better!" Mikey retorted. "At least it was an idea – I haven't noticed you coming up with any at all!"

He was right, and Leo forced himself to calm

down a bit. "Sorry," he said. "I'm wound up."

"Yeah." Mikey stood up and went to the window. "And now I've seen it for myself, I'm pretty wound up, too. I thought – well, I hoped – that you were making some of this up. Exaggerating, you know. But you're not. It *is* seriously weird."

"So what are we going to do?"

Mikey thought for a minute. "I think I ought to go home and e-mail Scott," he said at last. "I'll tell him what's going on – as much of it as he'll believe, anyway – and see if he's heard anything else."

"Colorado's hours behind us," Leo pointed out. "He won't even be awake yet."

"Never mind; he'll get the message as soon as he gets up, and if I tell him it's urgent he'll reply straight away." Mikey paused. "Unless you want to tell him yourself?"

Leo shook his head. "Can't. Dad won't let me use the modem."

"Even if it's an emergency?"

Leo laughed hollowly. "Then I'd have to explain what the emergency was, wouldn't I?"

"Ah. Right. OK, then – I'll go home, and I'll ring you as soon as I hear anything."

"What am I supposed to do in the meantime?" Leo asked worriedly.

Mikey sighed. "Sit it out," he said. "I can't think of anything else. Sorry. Oh, and don't use your computer."

They mooched downstairs, not speaking. There wasn't anything else to say. The twins weren't anywhere around, but as they went through the hall, Mum called from the sitting-room.

"Leo! I meant to tell you. Dad and I'll be out tomorrow. It's an afternoon thing, and it's quite a long way away, but we should be back by about seven. I want you to look after Thomas and Tina, so don't go fixing up anything else, will you?"

"Tomorrow?" Leo said, aghast. He didn't want to be left on his own in the house!

"That's right." Mum appeared at the sitting-room door. "We'll have to leave straight after lunch, and – Oh. Hello, er. . ."

"Mikey," said Mikey, putting on a cheerful voice and face. "Hi, Mrs Banks. Actually, Leo was coming over to my house tomorrow. We're doing some work together on a school project. So if he's got to babysit, is it OK if I come over here instead?"

"Well, I suppose so," said Mum. "If you really want to put up with the twins. All right, then. I expect it'll be nice for Leo to have some company."

She went back into the sitting room, and Mikey whispered, "That's fixed, then. I'll phone you later." He opened the front door. "Good luck!"

And he biked away.

Waiting for Mikey to ring was a horrendous ordeal for Leo. The rest of the day dragged on endlessly, while his brain worried and nagged. Had Mikey said he'd only ring if there was some news from Scott? Or had he promised to call whatever happened? Leo couldn't remember. Should he phone Mikey or should he leave him alone? And if he did phone, should he do it now or leave it a bit longer?

In the end he didn't do anything, and by teatime he was as jumpy as a flea. He could have let off some steam by going to the Rec or the park, but he didn't dare leave the house in case he missed Mikey's call. His only consolation was that there hadn't been any more spooky happenings. Yet.

But if nothing actually *spooky* had happened, there were still some weird things going on. The twins, for instance. Since lunchtime, they'd been following him around wherever he went. They didn't pester him; in fact they didn't even say anything. They just followed. And they *stared*. It was as if they knew something was in the wind, and they were waiting for the fun to start. It made Leo very, very edgy.

And then there were the spiders. They were small and perfectly ordinary spiders, and they weren't doing anything sinister. It was just that there were so many of them around. One in the kitchen (he found out about that when Mum yelped). One spinning a little web inside a lampshade. One making another web in a corner of the bathroom ceiling. And a black, hairy one in the bath. Three times Dad put that one out of the window, and each time it – or one just like it – was back within twenty minutes. It must have come up the pipe and through the plug hole, Leo thought. *Incy Wincy Spider, climbing up the spout. . .*

There were hundreds of spiders in the garden again, too. Or so Dad said, but neither Leo nor Mum felt like going to see for themselves. Mum was starting to get quite paranoid, and Leo didn't blame her.

They were half way through tea when the phone rang. Leo leaped for it as if he were on springs, and with huge relief he heard Mikey's voice at the other end.

"Leo? Anything happened?"

"Not yet," said Leo. "All quiet so far."

"Well, that's something. Listen, I've just heard back from Scott. That friend of his whose folks moved away suddenly – Scott got a letter from him. Not an e-mail, an ordinary letter. The guy says he's never, ever going to have anything to do with computers ever again. And he told Scott something else."

"What?" said Leo eagerly.

There was a pause. Then: "I don't know if I ought to tell you this. . ."

"You've got to!"

"Well, OK; I suppose I have. What happened to him was almost exactly what's been happening to you. I mean, right down to the details. He got rid of the bugged Incy Wincy game, but the spider was still there. It started leaving threatening messages, then tonnes of cobwebs started appearing all over the place."

"What did he do about it?" Leo asked.

Mikey gave a hollow laugh. "You're not going to like this, either. He tried to do what I did this morning."

"You mean, talk back to it?"

"Yeah. He typed in a whole load of insults – everything he could think of. Nothing showed up on screen, same as with us. But the message must have got through. And Incy Wincy didn't like it, 'cause that was when things started turning *really* nasty."

Leo felt as if his stomach had sunk into his feet. "Oh, God!" he said.

Mikey made a noise that might have been a nervous gulp. "Look," he said, "I didn't really *insult* it. I only typed 'Get lost'. I mean, no one could really get riled at that, could they? Not if they're the least bit. . ."

The words tailed off as he realized what he had been about to say. "Reasonable?" Leo finished for him. "Oh, sure. And of course, this thing is amazingly reasonable, isn't it?"

There was a silence. Then Mikey said in a small voice, "Sorry, Leo. But I didn't *know*. . ."

The tea that Leo had been eating was churning up his stomach and making him feel sick. He couldn't blame Mikey, though. How could Mikey have known?

"All right," he said, struggling to sound calm. "It's not your fault. Look – did Scott tell you anything else? Anything that might help?"

"No," said Mikey. "But he's promised to do some more digging. I should have another e-mail from him by tomorrow morning."

If I can last out till then, Leo thought. But he didn't say it.

"OK," he replied. "Then we'll just have to wait, won't we? There's nothing else we can do."

And his mind silently added: *Just as long as tomorrow isn't too late. . .*

13

The evening wasn't a good one for Leo. Nothing actually *happened*, but in a lot of ways he'd have felt much better if it had. At least then he'd have known what he was up against – and he would have had Mum and Dad in the house. But Incy Wincy didn't work like that. He was going to bide his time. He was going to wait till Mum and Dad were well out of the way.

He wasn't going to make his move till tomorrow.

Before he went to bed that night, Leo unplugged his computer and pulled every single lead out of its socket, leaving the cables lying on the floor like a pile of spaghetti. He also took the toy spider that Thomas and Tina had pinched from playschool, and put it in the dustbin.

The twins didn't know he'd done that. Even if they had, he didn't think they'd have cared. They were still following him everywhere, but apart from that they were being very good – so good that even Dad had noticed and was puzzled. When Leo got into bed and switched his light off, there wasn't a sound from their room. No chanting, no singing, no giggling. Thomas and Tina, it seemed, were happy to wait for Incy to make the next move.

To his own surprise, Leo got to sleep quickly and easily, and didn't have any bad dreams. He woke up at something like his usual time, and yawned and stretched as he opened his eyes.

Then froze as he saw what was written on the ceiling, in a grey festoon of cobwebs.

NOT LONG NOW

He should have known that Incy wouldn't let him off the hook completely. The chance for just one more wind-up before the big attack must have been too tempting to resist.

Heart pounding, Leo climbed on to his desk and wiped the cobweb message away with a scrunched-up T-shirt. It had completely wrecked his efforts to calm himself down, and by the time he finished he felt as if he'd been wired up to an electricity pylon, with about eight zillion volts buzzing through his nerves.

Downstairs, he found the twins in the hall. They were crawling along the floor with their noses close to the skirting-board, but they stopped when they saw Leo.

"'Lo, Leebo," said Thomas. "We're being 'piders."

Leo's stomach gave a queasy lurch.

"Yeah," said Tina. "'Piders looking for somefing." She rose to her knees and waggled her fingers menacingly. "'Piders looking for *you*! *Yum-yum-yum!*"

Leo ran into the kitchen, wondering how he was going to stand the strain of waiting till Mikey arrived.

Mikey phoned later in the morning. He'd heard back from Scott. But if Leo had hoped Scott would come up with something helpful, he was in for a disappointment.

"He can't get hold of the guy who moved away," Mikey told him. "So it looks like we're on our own." He was trying to sound cheerful and upbeat, but Leo wasn't fooled.

"I'll be over about two," Mikey added. "And

I'll bring some of my programs – they might come in handy. Hope so, anyway." He laughed. Or tried to. "See you later, OK?"

At lunch, Leo could hardly eat a thing. He made himself force down a few mouthfuls, to stop Mum from becoming suspicious, but his brain was fixed firmly on what lay ahead. The most nerve-racking thing was not knowing what Incy was planning – or, even, what he was capable of. It could be that all the threats were just one big bluff, and the worst Incy could do was produce a tonne or two of cob-webs. In which case Leo and Mikey would have made prize idiots of themselves, and that would be that.

But Leo didn't think they'd be so lucky. He had a feeling in his bones that they hadn't seen the half of what Incy could do. Not yet. But they would. Today's message had told him that.

Not long now. . .

Thomas and Tina had been tearing around all morning, so by the time Mum and Dad left, they were yawning and ready for an afternoon nap. Mum put them to bed and told Leo not to let them sleep for more than an hour, or they'd play up in the evening. Leo watched the car drive away. Then he tiptoed up to the twins' room, and shut the door properly. They couldn't reach the handle to open it. No way did he want them under his feet this afternoon. Like it or lump it, they could stay where they were. It was *safer*.

He paced round the house, counting minutes impatiently, until after what seemed like ages Mikey arrived on his bike. He had a bag slung over his shoulder, and as he dumped it on the hall table he said, "I think I've remembered everything."

Leo stared at the bulging bag. "What's *in* there?"

"Tools, mostly." Mikey started to pull them out. "Screwdrivers, pliers, wire-strippers . . . and this."

"A *hammer*?"

"Well, you never know, do you? Oh, and a couple of computer programs I've invented."

"What are you going to do with all this?" Leo asked.

"Well, for starters, I want to take the lid off your computer and have a look inside," said Mikey. "Just to make sure there's nothing funny going on in there. After that – depends what we find, I suppose."

Leo wondered what he expected to find, but he couldn't bring himself to ask. Mikey was all bright and breezy and cheerful today – almost too cheerful, as if he was covering up for something. Leo could guess what it was, and admired him. It must take a lot of guts, he thought, to overcome a phobia and face the thing you were scared of. It made him feel ashamed of his own fear – and it also made him determined not to be a chicken any more.

Going in to his room with someone else was much easier than going in on his own. He could even dare to switch on the computer, if Mikey wanted him to. Though he hoped Mikey wouldn't. . .

They'd brought Dad's modem with them, but Mikey didn't plug it in. He just plonked himself on the bed and said, "So what are we going to do while we wait?"

Leo looked at him blankly. "Do?"

"Sure! We can't just sit here and twiddle our thumbs, can we? Got any games – Monopoly or Cluedo or something?"

Board games weren't Leo's thing at all. But he did have an old Jenga set that he hadn't used for centuries, so he dug it out and they set up the tower of interlocking wooden blocks on the floor. The idea was to build the tower higher at the top by taking pieces out from the bottom, until someone pulled out one too many and the whole thing fell over. Mikey's hand was much steadier than Leo's, and he won three games in a row. They were just starting on a fourth game when there was a noise from the twins' room.

"Oh-oh!" said Leo. "They're awake."

"So what?" Mikey shrugged. "Leave them to it. If they can't get out, they can't bother us."

Leo had shut and locked the window, so no chance of accidents there. Mikey was right. The twins were safe enough.

But they weren't quiet for very long. A couple of minutes later Leo heard their door being thumped. Then:

"Leebo! LEE-bo!"

Bang, bang. "LEEEE-BO!! We want to come out!"

"Ignore 'em," Mikey suggested.

Leo wavered. If he didn't answer at all, the twins would think there was no one else in the house, and then they'd get scared.

BANG-THUMP-BANG . . . "*LEEE-BO!!*"

It was no use. With a sigh, Leo got up and went out of the room. Outside the twins' door he called out, "You can't come out!" Then he added a lie: "Mum said you've got to stay there!"

No answer. Leo frowned. "Thomas? Tina?

Did you hear what I said?"

Still nothing. Were the twins all right?

He started to open the door — then stopped as he heard a stifled giggle on the other side.

"Oh, *right*!" he said crossly. "I get it! Well, I'm not letting you out, and that's that!"

Someone on the other side of the door made a rude noise. Then, as Leo started to move away. . .

"*Leeee-booo!*" It was a high-pitched scream, and it nearly scared the life out of him. He whirled round, and for a moment stood frozen. Then he dived back to the twins' room and flung the door open.

The second shock was much worse. There were Thomas and Tina, sitting on the floor in the middle of an enormous mess of toys. They must have pulled absolutely *everything* out of their toy box.

And every single toy was draped in cobwebs. There were cobwebs draped on the walls and window too, like Christmas decorations at Castle Dracula. The twins had webs in their hair, making them look like two little grey gnomes. And they were grinning at Leo.

"What's up?" Mikey was coming along the landing. Leo glanced over his shoulder, and

Mikey stopped when he saw his face.

"It's started," Leo said in an unsteady voice. He stood aside from the door. Mikey looked.

"Oh, God!" He backed off and his face turned pale.

Thomas and Tina giggled again. Then they scrambled to their feet and dashed out of the room. Leo didn't try to stop them; he hardly even noticed as they ran away along the landing. Suddenly, all he wanted was to attack the cobwebs, clear them away, until the room was free of them! *That's the way to beat this!* his brain told him feverishly. *Get rid of the webs, just keep on getting rid of them, till Incy can't make any more! Come on, Leo – do it, now!*

"I'm going to get that room clean!" he said, through clenched teeth.

"What?" said Mikey.

"I want it clean! I've got to get that stuff out of here!"

Mikey called after him as he ran towards the stairs, but Leo took no notice. In the kitchen he grabbed pan, brush, cloths, rubber gloves – he couldn't bear the thought of touching those cobwebs! He didn't know where the twins were, but he didn't care. He just had to *do* this!

"Come on!" he said breathlessly to Mikey

when he pelted back upstairs. "Help me!"

Mikey looked faintly green as well now. "It isn't going to do any good!" he protested.

"It is! It's got to!" Leo started into the room. "Come *on*!"

But Mikey didn't follow him, and when Leo looked back he swallowed and said, "I can't. I just . . . can't go in there." Another gulp. "Sorry."

"Oh, hell! All right then, I'll do it! Go back to my room. See if you can think of something!"

It took Leo more than half an hour to clean all the spiders' webs away. As he worked, he was horribly jumpy, expecting at any moment to hear the scrabbling in the wall, or to see more webs start to appear. Nothing happened, though by the time he finished he was a bag of nerves. But at least the webs were gone.

"That's it!" He barged back into his own bedroom. "I've got rid of every single—" He stopped, staring. "What the heck are you *doing*?"

Mikey was on the floor – and so was Leo's computer. In pieces.

"I thought you were just going to take the cover off!" Leo said, aghast.

"I was." Mikey looked up at him. "But when

I did, I saw – mind you don't tread on that! – I saw something."

Leo's pulse sped up. "What?"

Mikey had a strange expression on his face. "I'm not quite sure," he said slowly. "I'm even starting to wonder if I imagined it. But . . . I thought there was something in there. Something that moved."

Leo was silent for a few moments. Then: "H-how big was it?" he asked.

"Like that." Mikey held up a finger and thumb. The gap between them was about the size of a very large spider.

"I'm glad you're here," Mikey went on in a small voice, "'cause you see, I took half the bits out of the computer, but I . . . sort of can't make myself look *right* inside it. Here." He pointed with a screwdriver. His hand was shaking. "And if I *did* see what I thought I did. . ."

"Right." Leo was feeling pretty squeamish too, but he could face it. Just. "Tell me what to do," he said. "And—"

He stopped, and whipped his head round to stare at the door.

Mikey tensed. "What is it?"

"Dunno. I thought. . ." The door was shut. And in the narrow gap underneath it, Leo could have sworn he'd glimpsed a shadow. As if something was moving along the landing floor.

"It's the twins, I expect." But he couldn't quite make himself believe it. The twins were always noisy, and this had been silent. "It's OK," he said firmly. "There's nothing to worry about. Nothing out there."

Is there?

"I think," he said, "I'd better look. Just in case."

He felt sick as he went to the door. For a couple of seconds he listened. No sound. He must've imagined it.

He opened the door. Looked out. And his eyes bulged.

"Oh, my God!" he whispered.

14

It wasn't possible. It couldn't have been done in the few minutes since Leo had last looked out here.

But it had. There it was, at the far end of the landing – a thick wall of grey webbing, that stretched from floor to ceiling, blocking the way to the stairs.

Leo stared, his mouth working like a stranded fish's. Then from behind him came a wail.

"Ooohhhh, Leoooo!" Mikey had come to the door and seen the web for himself. He wasn't just green now – he was grey as well. Through chattering teeth he stammered,

"Oh, no! Oh, no, no, *no*!"

A hideous thought crashed into Leo's head. He hadn't set eyes on the twins since they'd run out of their bedroom. Where *were* they? Upstairs somewhere? Or – or –

"Mikey!" He snatched hold of Mikey's arm. "I don't know where Thomas and Tina are! You've got to help me find them!"

Mikey shook his head wildly. "I c-can't! I can't go n-n-near that thing!"

"But—"

"I said, I *can't*!" Mikey yelled. They looked at each other for a moment, and Leo saw how truly terrified Mikey was. He couldn't argue with him. There wasn't time.

He whirled round and ran along the landing. Behind him, Mikey slammed the bedroom door, but Leo didn't even notice. He reached the web, took a deep breath and launched himself straight at it.

He plunged into what felt like an enormous, elastic candy-floss. Sticky strands curled round his arms and legs, and more clung to his face, making him splutter and gasp. Leo's stomach churned at the horrible sensation, but he battled on, feeling cautiously for the top step of the stairs. If he missed his footing and fell. . . But he mustn't think about that; mustn't think what it would be like to pitch headlong into this thick grey fog and be swallowed up and engulfed by it.

His foot found the edge of the top stair, but he didn't dare move any further. He couldn't see where he was going; everything around him was grey, and the greyness was getting denser and darker. He'd thought the web would only be a few centimetres deep but he was wrong. How far *did* it go? he asked himself. It couldn't – surely it couldn't – reach all the way down the stairs, and into the hall . . . or even further? Suppose there was no end to it? Suppose that somehow he'd find himself trapped in another world, another dimension, made of nothing but endless spiders' webs?

Leo started to panic. He stumbled back, fighting against the sticky strands that tried to hold on to him. He couldn't find the edge of the web! He opened his mouth to yell, "Help!" but all he got was a mouthful of goo. He couldn't get free! He'd never get free! He was stuck here, and – and –

With a gasp he broke out of the clinging mesh and tottered several steps backwards along the landing before he managed to stop himself. There was a hole in the web where he'd torn it, and wispy tentacles waved menacingly at him. Leo gasped for breath, wiping the vile stuff from his face.

Then, from somewhere below, he heard a faint cry.

"*Leee-bo!*"

"Thomas?" Leo's heart gave an enormous, painful lurch of fright. "Tina?"

"*Leeboooo! Don't like it!*"

Oh, God! Leo thought. "Thomas!" he yelled. "Kids, where *are* you?"

A thin, distant wail answered him. "*I want Muuuummy!*"

Horrified, Leo flung himself at the web again. But this time he couldn't force his way more than an arm's length into it before it pushed him back like an elastic wall. He couldn't get to the twins. He didn't even know where they were. All he could hope and pray was they were somewhere the web hadn't reached. That they weren't snared and tangled in it. *Yet.*

What to do? Leo's mind spun. There was no other way to get downstairs. Unless. . .

The drainpipe! It came to him like a lightning flash. The idea of climbing down the pipe was mad; he'd never done it, probably couldn't do it, but he had to try! *Incy Wincy Spider, climbing up the spout. . .*

"Hang on, kids, I'm coming!" he shouted into the web, and tore back towards his bedroom.

As he reached the door, it was jerked open from inside and Mikey came running out. He and Leo crashed into each other, and as they rebounded Mikey started to babble.

"Th-th-th . . . th-th-th. . ." His eyes were wild. "It's in th-th-th. . ."

Leo shoved past him, and stopped dead.

The window of his bedroom, too, was covered with grey. A fine film of cobweb stretched across the ceiling.

And the top of Leo's desk was veiled in sticky strands.

"Mikey!" Leo grabbed Mikey, shaking him roughly. "Mikey, what happened? Did you see it happen? Did you see what made it?"

But Mikey couldn't answer. He was gibbering like a maniac, and the harder Leo tried to shake him out of it, the worse it got. He had to be brought back to his senses – and Leo remembered all the old movies he'd seen. A sharp shock, that was it! There was a vase of flowers on the landing. He grabbed it, pulled the flowers out, and as Mikey burbled in terror, Leo threw the whole vaseful of water over his head.

Mikey rocked back on his heels as the water hit him. He yelped and spluttered – but the panicky wailing stopped as if a switch had been thrown. Dripping, blinking, he stared at Leo.

"Oh, God!" he whispered. "Where *was* I?"

Leo didn't bother to answer that. "Mikey," he urged, "you've got to help me now! The twins are stuck downstairs, and I'm going to try. . ."

His voice tailed off as he saw something.

Some of the water he'd thrown had scattered into his bedroom. It had splashed on the edge of a cobweb . . . and made a hole in it.

Water! Would it work on the big web? Would it break it up enough for him to get through?

"Quick!" he said to Mikey. "Get anything that'll hold water! Come *on*!"

Mikey didn't understand, but he'd recovered enough to do what he was told. Together they ran to the bathroom and started to fill up every container they could find – the vase, tooth-mugs, plastic waste-bin – *anything*.

"Come on!" Leo shouted again. Lugging as much as they could carry, they stumbled along the landing.

"One – two – *three*!" A cascade of water hurtled at the web.

And a gaping hole dripped soggily in the middle of the dense wall.

"*It works!*" With Mikey at his heels, Leo pelted back to the bathroom to refill the containers. They flung two more lots at the web, making the hole bigger each time.

But when they came back with the third lot, Mikey noticed something.

"Leo," he hissed. "It's mending itself."

Somehow, the web was putting itself back together. Already the hole they'd made had shrunk to half its size.

"We're not fast enough." Mikey's voice was hollow, and he'd started to shiver. "We need a firefighter's hose to get through it. And we haven't got one. . ."

Leo knew he was right. "But we've got to try!" he said desperately. "We've got to get to the twins!" Suddenly he remembered his first idea. "Look – I'm going to try and climb down the drainpipe! If I can do it, then get back into the house from ground level. . ."

"That's crazy!" Mikey protested. "You'll break your neck!"

"Have you got a better idea?" Leo demanded.

He didn't expect a reply, but suddenly Mikey's expression hardened. "Yeah," he said. "I have."

"What?"

Mikey gulped. "I don't know for sure if I can do it," he said. "First, it's a gamble and it might not even work. And second, I don't know if I've got the guts." Another gulp. "But it's better than the drainpipe idea. And if you can do that – well, I'm not going to let myself chicken out." He made a brave effort to grin. "Got to try, haven't I?"

Leo's pulse was pounding. "What're you going to do?"

"I'm going to put your computer back together. Then I'm going to get on the Internet, and download that Incy Wincy Spider game all over again. And then – " Mikey squared his shoulders – "then I'm going to play the game. And I'm going to try and *kill* that spider!"

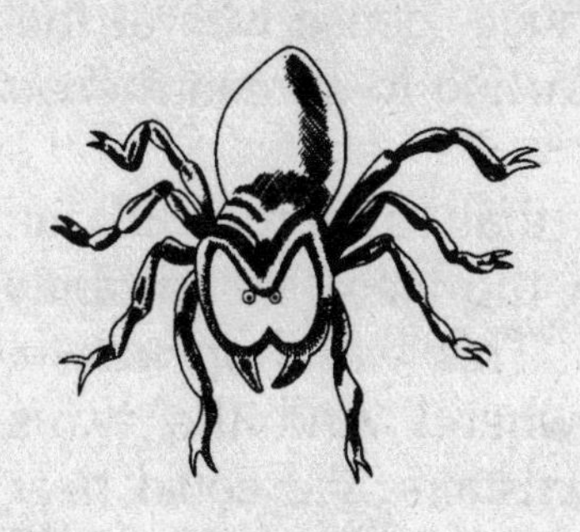

15

"Come on, come *on*!" Leo flung another vaseful of water at his bedroom window. "It's spreading faster – I can't keep it at bay much longer!"

"I'm *trying*!" Mikey yelled back. He was feverishly untangling plugs and cables. "Another minute, that's all!"

Leo tore past him and back to the bathroom. He hardly knew where to throw the next vaseful, because the webs were *everywhere* now. In his bedroom. In the twins' room. Probably in Mum and Dad's room too, though he hadn't dared look. The only place they hadn't appeared was the bathroom.

And the huge, dense web at the top of the stairs was starting to spread menacingly along the landing.

He made that his target this time. A hole appeared in the web, but instantly started to mend itself. This was hopeless – he wasn't getting anywhere! And the twins were still trapped downstairs. He could hear them crying, but there was nothing he could do to help them!

As he tore to the bathroom again, a yell came from the bedroom. "Leo! I'm switching on *now*!"

One glance into the room showed Mikey, white-faced and shaking, crouched on Leo's chair and staring fixedly at the computer screen. The computer was starting up, bleeping and whirring. There was no sign of Incy Wincy Spider on the screen, but the web across the window, which Leo had soaked with water only a minute ago, was back. And it was getting *bigger*.

"Get it away from me!" Mikey said through clenched teeth. "Please, Leo! *Please!*"

Leo poured the next three lots of water over the web, and over the creeping strands that were spreading further into the room. Though Mikey was still shaking with fright, it helped.

But it wouldn't help for long.

Dashing for the bathroom once more, Leo saw the screen change as Mikey connected to the Internet. For a moment he felt a lurching doubt. What if Mikey was wrong? What if this was the biggest mistake they could possibly make? They had no proof that it would work.

"Mikey—" he began.

"Quiet!" hissed Mikey. "I've got to concentrate. Just keep those webs away from me!"

He slammed a disk into the computer's floppy drive and his fingers flew on the mouse buttons. "Come-on-come-on-come-on! *Yeah!* Got it!"

Leo didn't stop to ask what he'd got. He had to trust that Mikey knew what he was doing. There was no other choice.

As he came running back with the next lot of water, he heard a horribly familiar sound from the speakers.

Bleep! Biddle-iddle-URP! It was the noise that announced Incy Wincy Spider. Vase in hand, Leo froze, gawping at the screen, till Mikey snapped furiously, "*Keep going!*"

The web was starting to creep across the carpet. Leo drenched it (God alone knew what Mum would say, but he couldn't care less about that now), then raced for more. When he returned, the computer game was down-loading on to his machine. *Whirr . . . beep . . . chug . . .* Gaudy colours flickered and flashed on the screen. And then, in garish red letters, came the message:

All done! Now you can start exploring Incy Wincy's web! Just click GO.

Leo and Mikey looked at each other. There was a pause. Then Mikey said, "Yeah?"

Leo swallowed, and nodded. "Yeah."

Mikey clicked GO.

And in the middle of the screen, Incy Wincy appeared.

The howl of laughter that blared out of the speakers almost made Leo jump out of his skin. It was horrible – a demented cackling that sounded completely mad and hideously triumphant. Above the jiggling cartoon spider, words appeared – HAHAARR, HAHAARR, INCY'S GOING TO GET YOU NOW!

"Oh no he's not!" said Mikey savagely. One hand slammed on the mouse button, and with the other he started to type.

GET LOST! DROP DEAD! GET KNOTTED! WE'RE NOT SCARED OF YOU!

As Mikey's words appeared, Leo's eyes bulged. "Mikey, no!" he shouted. "You'll only make it madder!"

"That's what I'm *trying* to do!" Mikey yelled back. "Challenge it – make it so furious that it loses its temper and screws up! And if my program works—"

"What? What if it works?"

"Then it'll – *ah*! Oh, no you don't!" His fingers flew again as the spider swelled to three times its size and loomed at him with teeth clashing like a buzz-saw. Incy shrank back, muttering and waggling his legs. He stopped still. Then he grinned, and a new message appeared on the screen.

OK, GUYS – IF YOU REALLY *WANT TO PLAY DIRTY. . .*

"This is it," said Mikey grimly. "Game on. Keep chucking that water, Leo. Things could get a bit hairy from here!"

Three more times Leo came sprinting back with more water. Then, returning with a fourth vaseful, he stared at the window in horror.

The web was getting bigger. It stretched half way across the floor now, and new tendrils were appearing in every corner. The water wasn't working any more!

He looked wildly at Mikey. Mikey hadn't seen the web; all his attention was locked on the computer. A pulsing, multicoloured maze had appeared on the screen, and chasing each other around the maze were Incy and what looked like a very small fly. Mikey was controlling the fly, Leo realized – and he was having a hard time keeping it out of reach of Incy's gnashing jaws.

Leo had to ask. He *had* to. "Wh-what happens if he catches the fly?"

Mikey didn't glance up. He just said tersely, "Game over."

"And then what?"

"*I don't know!*" Mikey hunched over mouse and keyboard, clicking and typing frenziedly. Words were hurtling all over the screen but they didn't make much sense – things like *BLAM!* and *AAARGH!* and *BLURRRGH!* as the spider and the fly rocketed around the maze.

"Get bigger!" Mikey yelled, thumping the mouse. "Come on, come on, *do* it!"

The fly juddered. It bounced, and its shape started to break up on the screen. Leo gasped—

Then suddenly Mikey let out a yell of triumph. The fly was whole again – and it was as big as the spider. Its eyes rolled and a buzzing like a gargantuan bluebottle came from the speakers.

"Yeah!" Mikey shrieked. "*Now* we'll get him!"

Incy jumped and gnashed, and the words *GET YOU, GET YOU!* flashed electric blue. But the fly was dodging through the maze again. It scooted down a side turning and came up on Incy from behind. . .

BAM! The word and the noise exploded together, and Leo jumped so hard that he bit his tongue. Where the two creatures had been was just a puff of cartoon smoke. And everything had gone quiet.

Trembling, Leo whispered, "Wh-where are they?"

Mikey didn't answer. He waited, fingers poised. Still nothing happened.

But then. . .

HAHAHAAAR! There was a burst of music, and Incy appeared again. And at the same moment, Leo heard something else.

"*Leee-booooo!*" It was a wail of sheer terror. And on its heels, echoing from somewhere on the floor below, came a deep, long-drawn *scri-i-i-itch*.

"The twins!" Horror punched through Leo. He'd forgotten all about Thomas and Tina – but they were still downstairs, still trapped! And something was happening down there!

"Leo, don't!" Mikey shouted as Leo dashed for the door. "It's too dangerous!"

"I can't leave them there!" Leo yelled back. Outside, on the landing, the web pulsed menacingly at him. It looked thicker and darker than ever, but Leo didn't hesitate. He launched himself straight at it, plunging into the sticky tangle of threads.

For a moment he thought he wouldn't do it. The web resisted, springing and bouncing like rubber bands. Leo clawed at it with all his strength – and suddenly it gave way in front of him. With a yelp he went tottering down the stairs. He grabbed the banister rail; it stopped him from falling, but it couldn't stop his staggering run. He crashed chaotically through the web, reached the foot of the stairs and went sprawling flat on his face in the hall.

He was clear of the strands. He raised himself on his elbows. Looked up.

And screamed.

"*Lee-booo!*" It was no more than a pitiful, muffled wail. It couldn't be anything else. Because in front of him, suspended from the hall ceiling and turning slowly, gently, were Thomas and Tina. They were completely enmeshed in grey webbing, unable to struggle or even move. All they could do was wail, and stare at him with wide, terrified eyes.

"Kids!" Leo scrabbled to his feet and ran to

them. Or tried to. But he hadn't gone two steps before he felt something dragging at his feet and pulling him back.

He looked down. And saw the crawling grey tendrils that had snaked across the floor and wrapped themselves around his ankles.

"*Aaah!*" Leo tried to jump away from the stuff. But the web clung on, curling over his trainers, tugging, tightening. He felt as if he was wading in treacle. It was creeping up his legs, already half way to his waist – he couldn't break free! He was stuck!

"*Leebo!*" Thomas and Tina cried again. But Leo couldn't help them. His arms were pinned to his sides. The web was tangling in his hair. It wrapped him in a cocoon of sticky threads, and he felt the floor drop away under him as slowly, slowly, he was lifted into the air, to dangle helplessly beside his little brother and sister.

"Mikey!" Yelling was hard because the web kept getting in his mouth, but Leo tried. "*Mikey!*"

There was no answering shout, but from upstairs came another noise, shrill and piercing.

Biddle-iddle-URP! It was followed by a loud burst of Incy Wincy's signature tune. And following that, a peal of demented laughter.

It stopped, and for a few moments everything was ominously quiet. Leo could hear his own heart thumping, but that was all.

Until. . .

Scri-i-i-itch . . . scri-i-i-itch. . .

Something was moving further down the hall. Something *large*. And then, through the murky strands of web, Leo glimpsed it. He could only make it out as a vague blob, but its body was about three times the size of a football. And it seemed to have a lot of legs.

"No. . ." he whispered. "Oh, nooo . . . *MIKEYYYY*!"

Again, Mikey didn't answer. But the thing heard him.

And with big, slow steps, it started to move towards him.

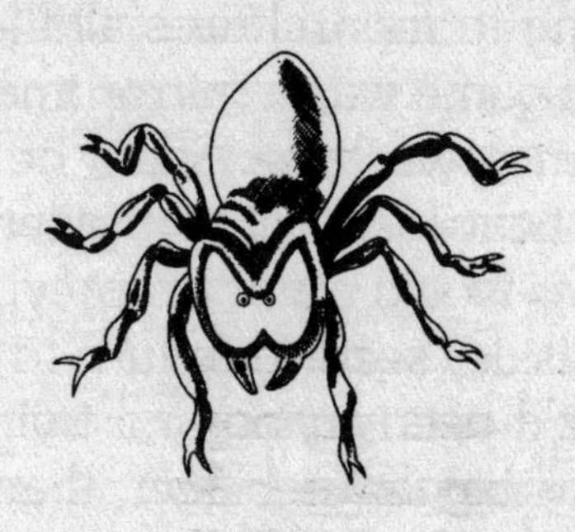

16

Mikey's eyes widened in horror as the three new flies appeared in the middle of the maze. They were only tiny little cartoon pictures. But there was no mistaking who they were supposed to be. The face of the biggest one even *looked* like Leo's. Three flies, caught in a spider's web. And the cartoon Incy Wincy was dancing and jiggling with glee, while the speakers cackled and speech-bubbles scribbled themselves across the screen:

HAHAARR, HAHAARR! YOU CAN'T HELP THEM NOW!!

Mikey had heard the twins wailing, and he'd heard Leo's scream. Now he knew what must be happening to them. It was all there, on the screen – the game was a mirror image of what was going on downstairs! And if he didn't win, if he didn't beat Incy Wincy Spider, then Incy Wincy Spider would claim his prey!

Mikey's insides seemed to turn to jelly at that thought. He'd been trying and trying to make his fly grow bigger – bigger than Incy, big enough to turn the tables, jump on the spider and squash it flat. But it wasn't *working*! He'd got something wrong, or missed a vital clue – he *had* to work out what he'd done wrong!

Then suddenly he saw that Incy was changing his tactics. He wasn't chasing Mikey's fly any more. Instead, he'd started off down another path of the maze.

A path that was leading him towards Leo and the twins. . .

"Oh, my God!" Mikey hissed. His fingers skittered on the computer controls, and his fly did a U-turn and buzzed along the maze after Incy. The Leo-fly started to squirm and wriggle as Incy got closer. Then the other two started as well. And from down below Mikey heard Thomas and Tina wail again.

"*NO!*" he yelled despairingly. *Come on, you wretched fly; get bigger, get BIGGER! Oh, why won't it? What's wrong*?

Then, like a bolt of inspiration, the answer slammed into his head.

Because spiders eat flies – but flies don't eat spiders! That was the secret of the game – to find another kind of creature – one that *could* beat Incy! But *how*?

Downstairs, in the tangles of the web, Leo saw the big, dark shape lurching towards him, and he yelled an echo of Mikey's: "No-o-o-o!" Upstairs, Mikey punched frantically at the computer controls. There must be something here that gave you a chance to win! But there wasn't. The thing was fixed so you *couldn't* beat Incy – that was the whole idea of the game!

Then he remembered the disk of his own, that he'd put into the machine when he started it up. What was on there? All the anti-virus stuff: that was no use. Other things, though – *ah*! There was a drawing and animation program! He'd made it himself, and though it wasn't exactly arty, it worked!

He pounced on the keyboard again, typing as fast as he could. A loud beep, and the pointer on the screen changed to something that looked like a paintbrush. Incy did a double-take. He jiggled and gnashed his teeth, and a snarl came from the speakers. But Mikey ignored it. He was drawing on the screen, drawing over the fly. It only took him a few seconds. And though Mikey wasn't very good at art, and the thing looked more like a budgie than the vulture it was meant to be, Incy Wincy got the message.

Mikey's fly had turned into a bird. And to the bird, Incy Wincy Spider looked like a *very* tasty morsel.

Incy jiggled again. He waved six of his legs. But suddenly it wasn't much of a threat any more.

"Hang on, Leo!" Mikey hissed through clenched teeth. The budgie-cum-vulture started to flap its wings. It started to move. And Mikey launched it through the maze, straight at Incy.

Incy tried to run. He scuttled straight for the three cartoon flies dangling in their web cocoons, but the bird was faster. It swooped and Incy reared up. . .

Downstairs, Leo and the twins screamed as the dark blob bulged towards them. They heard a snarl – then the snarl was drowned by a rushing, like a gale, or huge wings beating.

The computer speakers blared out an awful noise that was a mixture of squealing, squawking and tearing. A red star burst out from the middle of the screen, and turned into a single word, in scarlet letters –

SPLAT!

And in his trap, Leo cringed with shock as a vast shadow seemed to plummet from the ceiling, straight at the oncoming monster. It smashed down, and the *SPLAT* on the upstairs screen was, to him, a deafening explosion. The three cocoons were buffeted backwards. They swung wildly, turning Leo's stomach upside down – then the ceiling strands gave way, and Leo crashed to the floor in a tangle of arms and legs and sticky goo.

Then . . . silence. Leo lay flat on his face, winded. He was still tangled in the web and he didn't even try to move. Somewhere close by he could hear Thomas and Tina yelling, but the only thing he thought was: *If they're bawling like that, they must be OK*. Stupidly, he wanted to laugh. Or scream. Or just tell himself that none of this was actually *happening*.

He was giggling when Mikey came down and found him. There wasn't much left of the web on the staircase; most of it had already shrivelled and vanished. The web encasing Leo was shrivelling, too. But Mikey couldn't resist the temptation. He went to the kitchen, filled the biggest saucepan he could find with water, and tipped the lot over Leo's head.

"Hi," he said, as Leo sat up, spluttering and gasping. His grin stretched from ear to ear. "I fixed him."

"It was easy, really." Mikey shrugged nonchalantly, and ducked the cushion Leo threw at him. "No, honest," he went on more seriously. "It was all there in the game. The secret was, you had to play it and *win*. 'Cause if you didn't, that meant the spider was free to do whatever it liked – inside or outside the computer."

Leo shuddered. "What *was* it?" he said. "Do you know?"

Mikey shook his head. "I don't suppose anyone does, except maybe whoever started it up in the first place. But I tell you one thing: if anyone ever says to me again that something's too weird to be true, I'm going to laugh."

"Me, too."

Mikey looked over his shoulder towards the bedroom door. "How're the twins?"

"They're pretty much OK. Playing with Gondy, last time I looked."

Little kids were amazing, Leo thought. By the time he and Mikey had cleaned them up, Thomas and Tina had got over their terrors, and now, to them, the whole thing was just like a game again. Apart from those last bad minutes, they'd even – sort of – *enjoyed* it. And the bad minutes had been forgotten pretty quickly. Tina had announced that she thought it was all Leo's fault, and she didn't like him any more, and she wasn't going to play that game again, so there! Then she'd stamped on his foot, hard, to get her own back, and after that it seemed he was forgiven.

As for himself – well, Leo didn't really want to think about that. He wanted to do what Thomas and Tina had done, and try to forget the whole thing. He couldn't, of course. But like Mikey said, they'd never know what Incy Wincy *really* was. So it would be pretty moronic to put himself through hell by worrying about it. The spider – or whatever it had been – was gone. And this time, he knew it wouldn't come back. Not unless he was stupid enough to download another jinxed game. And that was something Leo was *not* going to do.

"Er. . . sorry about your computer, by the way," Mikey said.

"Oh. That." Leo looked at it. There was a scorch mark on the plastic case, showing where one of the main bits (he didn't know what it was called; that was Mikey's department) had gone phut as the spider was destroyed.

"It can . . . um . . . happen sometimes," Mikey added. "If there's a fault. At least, you can tell your dad that and he'll probably believe it."

"Yeah." Dad might or might not let him have a new computer. Leo didn't know, and right now he wasn't the least bit bothered. He could do without computers for a while. Quite a long while.

"What time're your folks coming home?" Mikey asked.

Leo shrugged. "About seven."

"Oh." Mikey looked at his watch. It was gone six. "You see, I just wondered what we're going to tell them. About all the water."

It slowly dawned on Leo that Mikey had a point. His room was soaking wet. The walls and carpet on the landing and down the stairs were soaking wet. And there was a huge great patch in the hall, where Mikey had chucked that last bowlful over him.

Suddenly, he started to giggle. Mikey blinked in surprise, but Leo couldn't make himself stop. He didn't know why, he couldn't even *begin* to work it out, but the idea of his parents coming home to find that the house had turned into a swimming pool was incredibly funny. In the end Mikey joined in – though he didn't know why, either – and the two of them hooted and hiccuped until, at last, the fit went away.

"We ought to do *something*," Mikey said, his face sobering.

"Yeah." Leo sighed. He stood up. He grinned. "Last one to the kitchen gets the mop that doesn't work!"

They dashed for the stairs together. Leo got there first, and in the kitchen he threw Mikey the mop with the handle the twins had broken when they were playing hobby-horses.

"Right, slave!" he said. "Get to work!"

"OK!" Mikey grimaced. Then he paused. "And if I find any spiders, I'll *yell*."

"Sure," said Leo. "But somehow, I don't think you will."

Are they ordinary animals – or are they **Creatures**?

To find out about other **Creatures** titles by **Louise Cooper** turn the page and read on

Creatures

Who's Been Sitting in My Chair?

"Opal!" Not knowing whether to feel relieved or annoyed, Rhoda started towards the armchair.

Then suddenly, in the cushioned depths of the chair's seat, a pair of eyes appeared.

There was nothing else. No face, no shape; just *eyes*. They were almond-shaped, amber-yellow, and had huge black pupils that glared furiously at Rhoda.

The purring stopped. There was an instant's absolute silence – then a piercing animal screech ripped through the room, an appalling din that battered Rhoda's ears. Her mouth opened in the beginnings of a terrified scream—

Creatures

See How They Run

He spun round. Behind him, on the floor, were six very large rats. They were sitting up on their haunches, front paws raised, staring at him.

Then he saw eight more in the doorway. These were smaller – more like normal size – but they were sitting up, too. Very still. Very quiet. *Staring*.

Jon swallowed. He moved the torch – and there were more rats, on a fallen beam that lay at a sloping angle between the ceiling and the floor. Lined in a row, sitting up, and absolutely motionless as they watched with their mean, beady little eyes.

The ugly truth dawned on Jon even before he started to swing the torch around in a wide arc. There were rats everywhere.

Creatures

If You Go Down to the Woods

"It's gone!" Caroly whispered. Her face was dead white and she looked as if she was going to be sick. "But how? It can't have *walked*!"

"Can't it?" said Alex. The horrible thought she had had earlier was creeping back. The owl. The fox. The bag. All those tracks in the snow.

And Chaz. . .

"They're coming alive," she said in a small, fearful voice. "The animals in our props and costume bits . . . They're *all* coming alive!"

Creatures

Atishoo! Atishoo! All Fall Down!

Turning away from the cage, Kel started to walk towards the door. The others followed.

And Chocky said, quite clearly, "Susie won't hurt *you*."

They all stopped dead. Turned. Stared. Birds can't grin, but if Chocky had been human there would have been a smirk on his face.

"Susie won't hurt *you*," he repeated, then paused as if he was thinking – or listening to something no one else could hear. "Susie *likes* you."

Creatures

Give a Dog a Bone

Chris bit his lip, then his shoulders heaved. "OK. But it sounds totally stupid. There's Nathaniel's statue, right? And Lancer's next to him. Well, I could see them both clearly from my window."

He hesitated again, then with an effort turned to face Pippa. He looked embarrassed. And he also looked frightened.

"I wasn't dreaming," he said, "and I didn't imagine it. The moon was out and the statues had shadows. The statue of Lancer was completely still; I mean, it's made of stone, so of course it was. But . . ." He swallowed. "Honest, Pippa, I'm not joking. Lancer's shadow was *moving*."